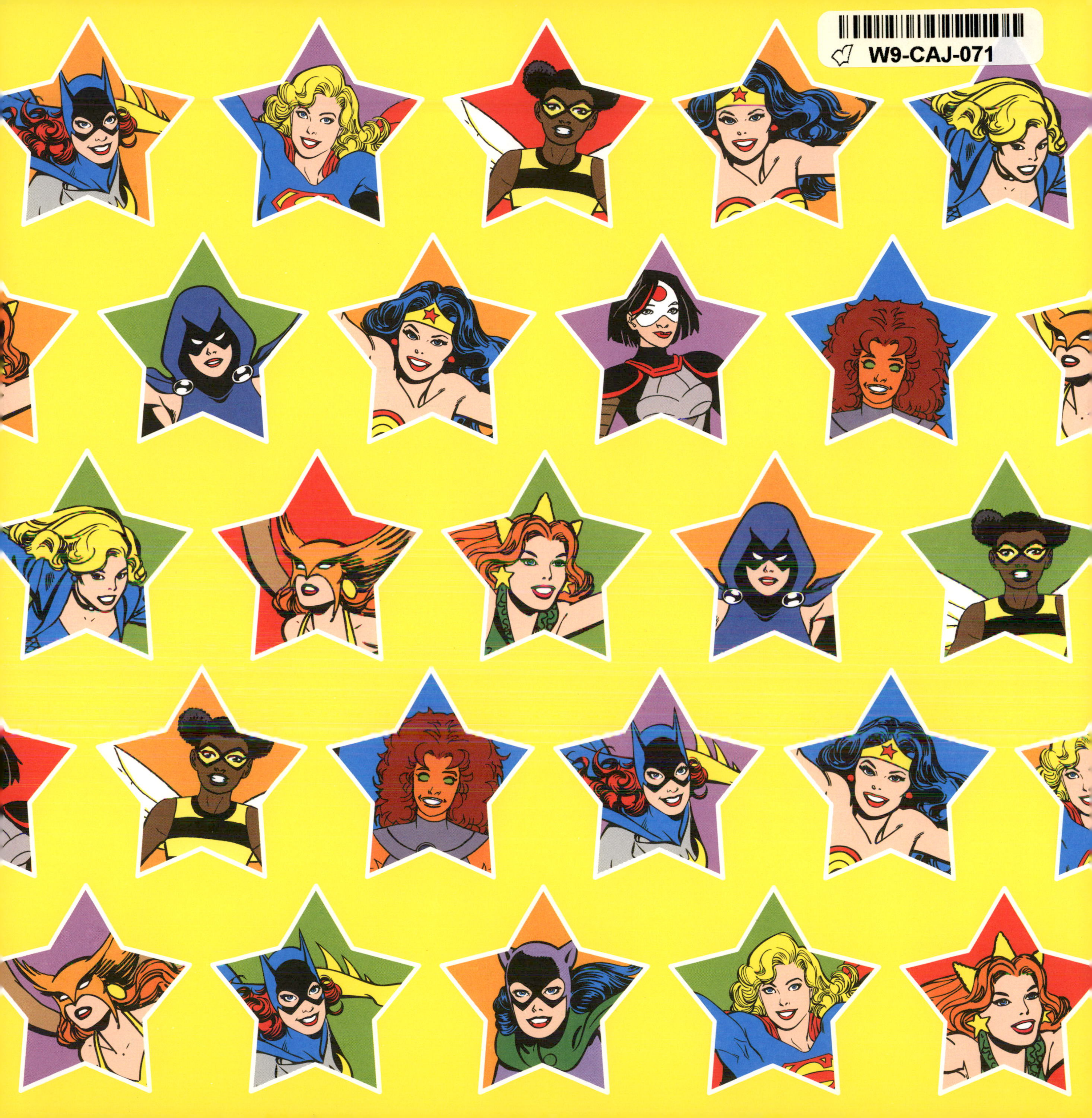

DC

THE BIG BOOK OF GIRL POWER

by Julie Merberg

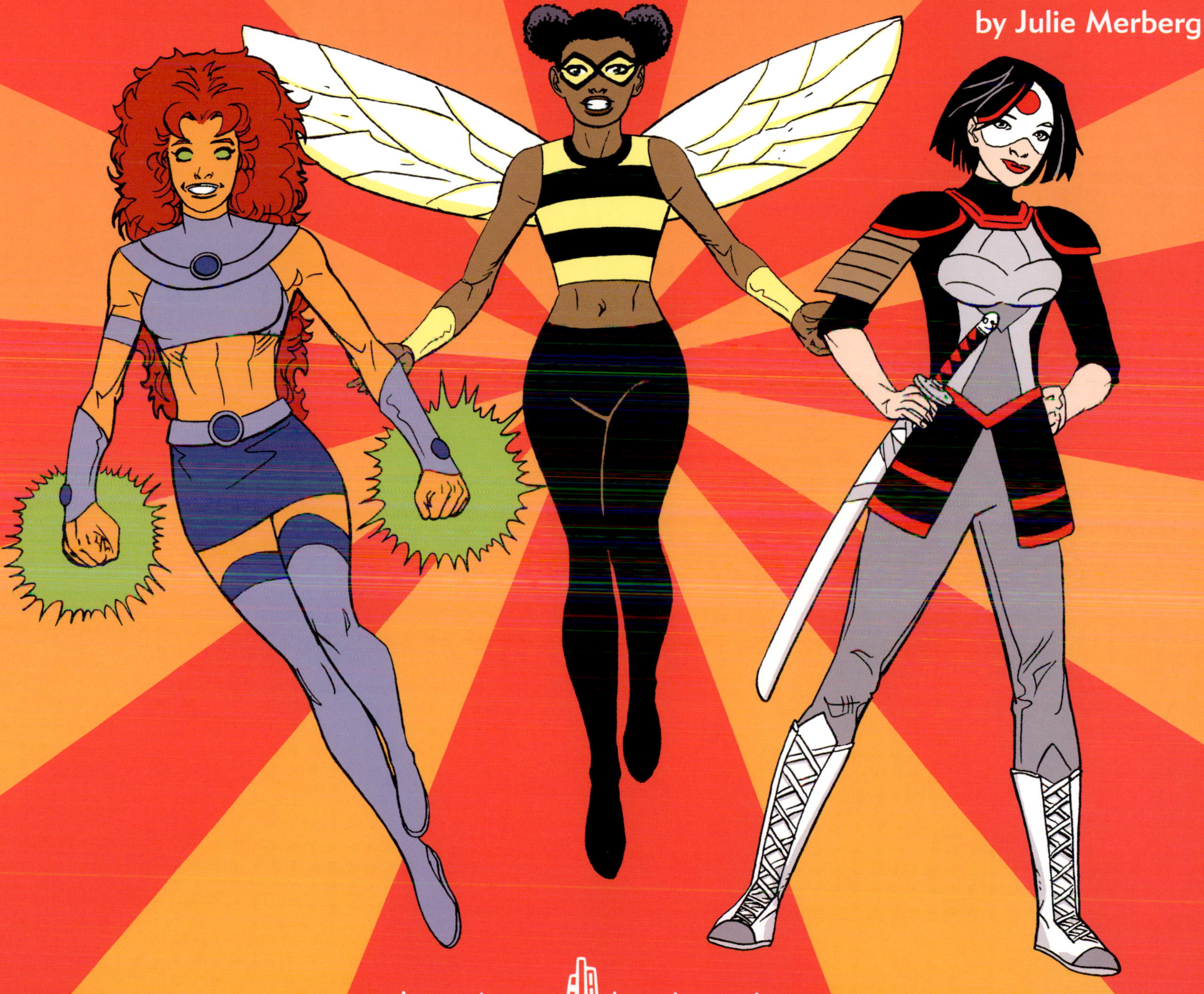

downtown bookworks

Downtown Bookworks Inc.
265 Canal Street
New York, New York 10013
www.downtownbookworks.com

Illustrations by Scott Kolins: pages 1; 8–11; 14–15 (background); 18–29;
and Bumblebee, Katana, and Starfire on page 32 and endpapers
Designed by Georgia Rucker
Typeset in Geometric and HouseShowcard

Printed in China
October 2018
ISBN 978-1-941367-23-0

10 9 8 7 6 5 4

INTRODUCTION

DC's super heroines are a powerful group. Some of them were born with special powers. Others worked really hard to master the skills that make them unbeatable. Many of them like to work together! What they all have in common is that they have the courage to fight for peace and justice. Turn the page to get to know them better.

WONDER WOMAN

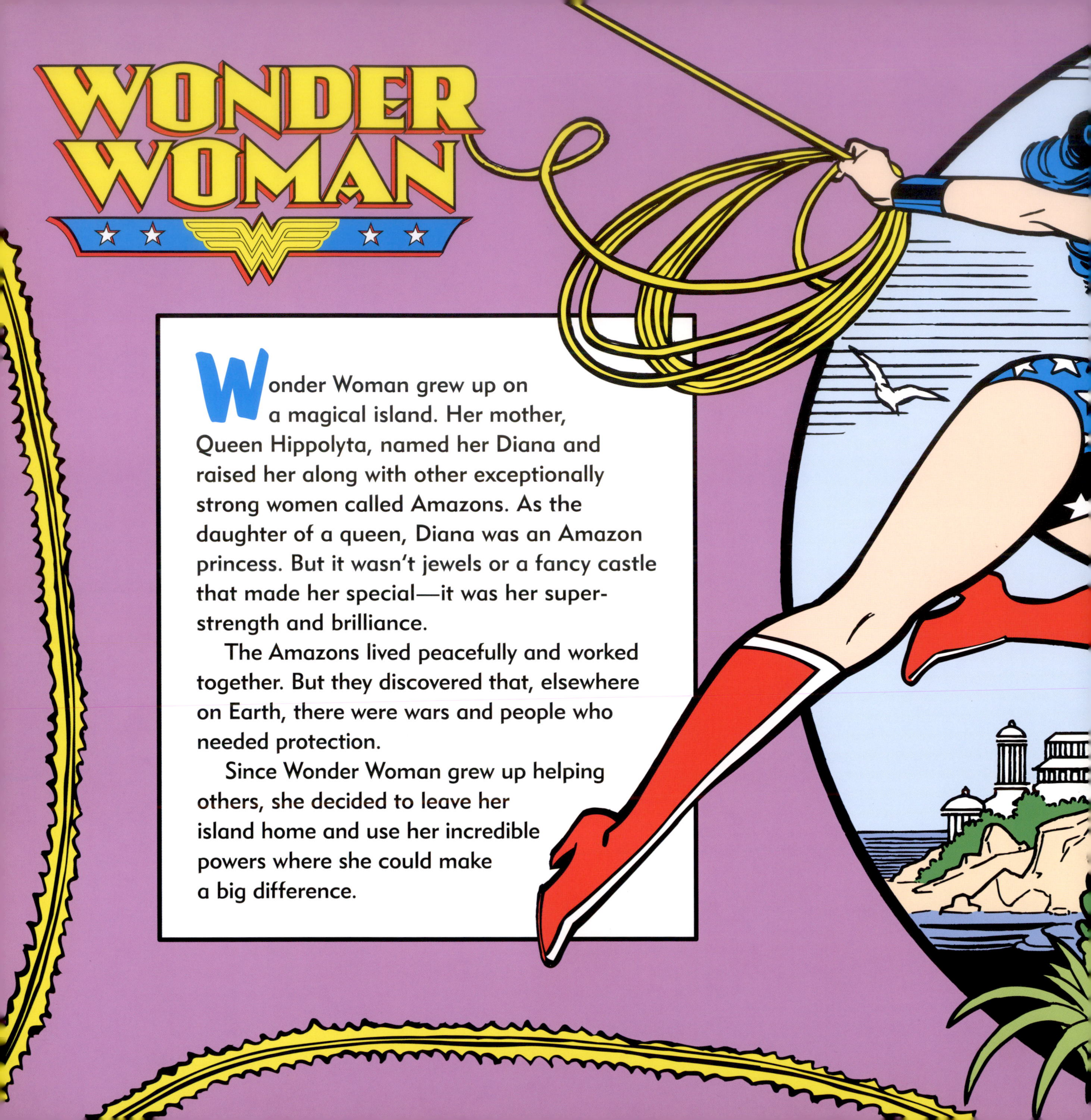

Wonder Woman grew up on a magical island. Her mother, Queen Hippolyta, named her Diana and raised her along with other exceptionally strong women called Amazons. As the daughter of a queen, Diana was an Amazon princess. But it wasn't jewels or a fancy castle that made her special—it was her super-strength and brilliance.

The Amazons lived peacefully and worked together. But they discovered that, elsewhere on Earth, there were wars and people who needed protection.

Since Wonder Woman grew up helping others, she decided to leave her island home and use her incredible powers where she could make a big difference.

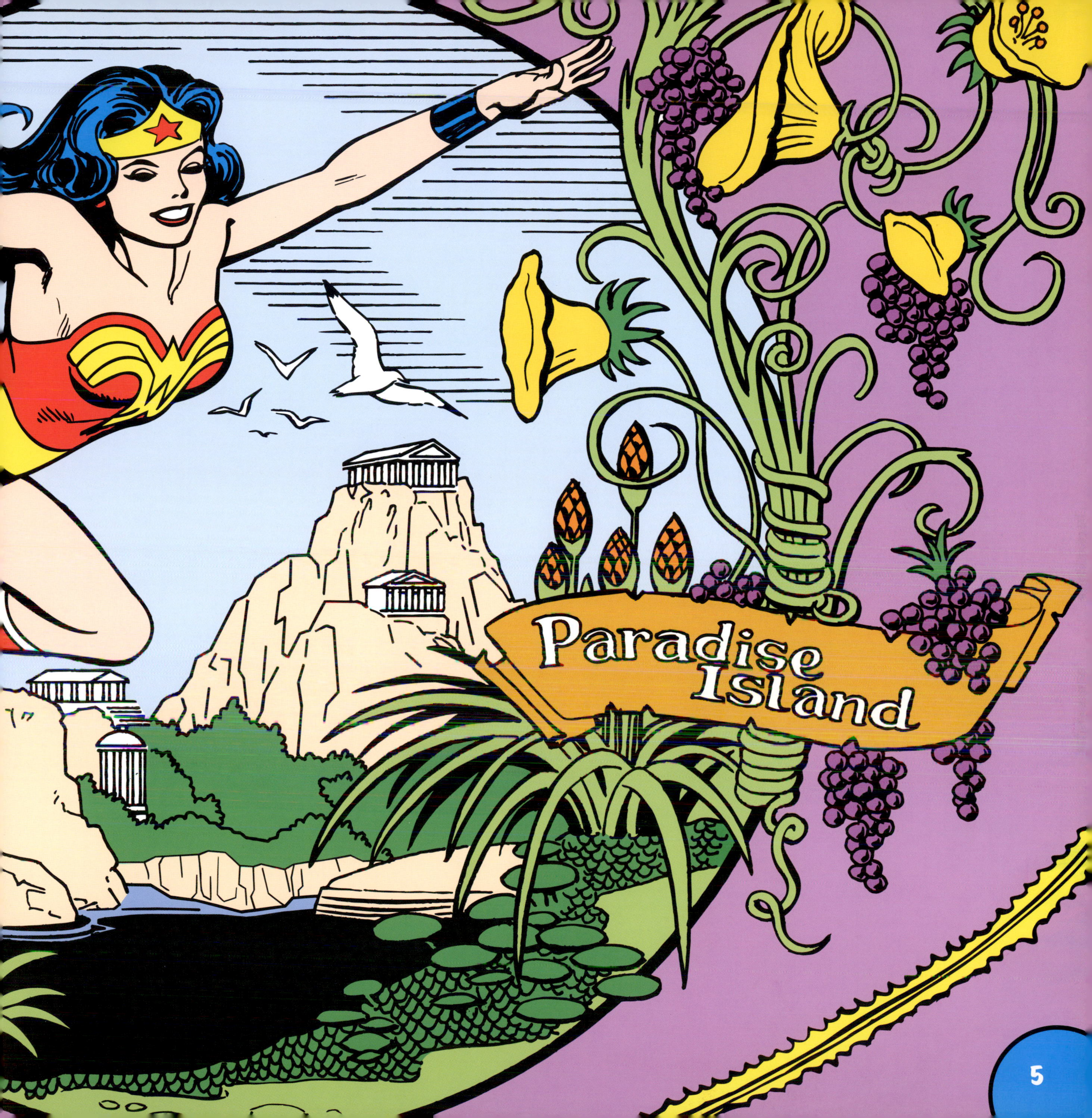
Paradise Island

WONDER WOMAN

Wonder Woman tries to make the world a more peaceful place to live. She has battled super-villains like Cheetah, Giganta, and Ares, the god of war. She forces criminals to follow the rules. And she uses her Golden Lasso to get people to tell the truth, because she knows how important it is to be honest.

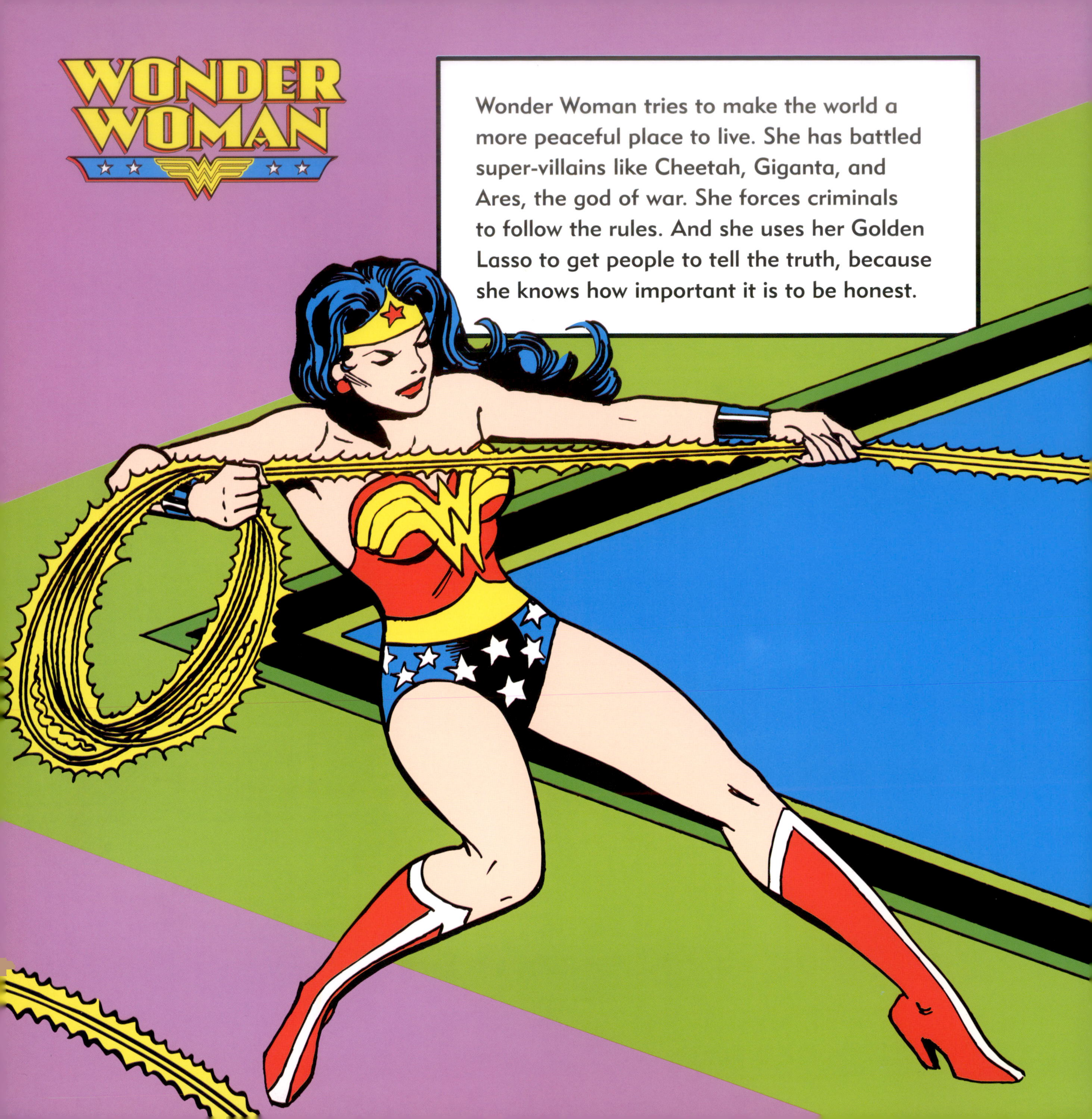

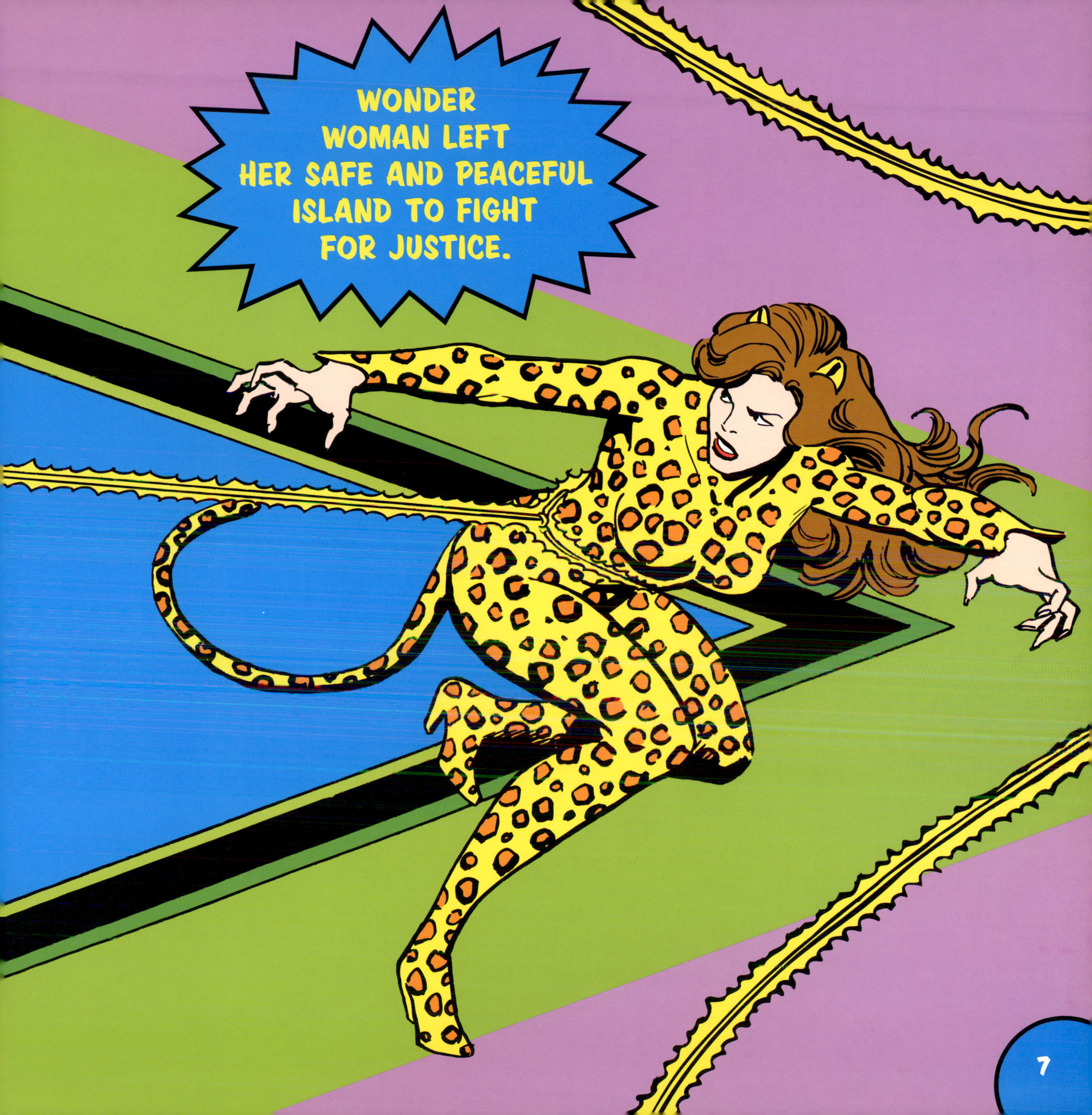
WONDER WOMAN LEFT HER SAFE AND PEACEFUL ISLAND TO FIGHT FOR JUSTICE.

HAWKGIRL

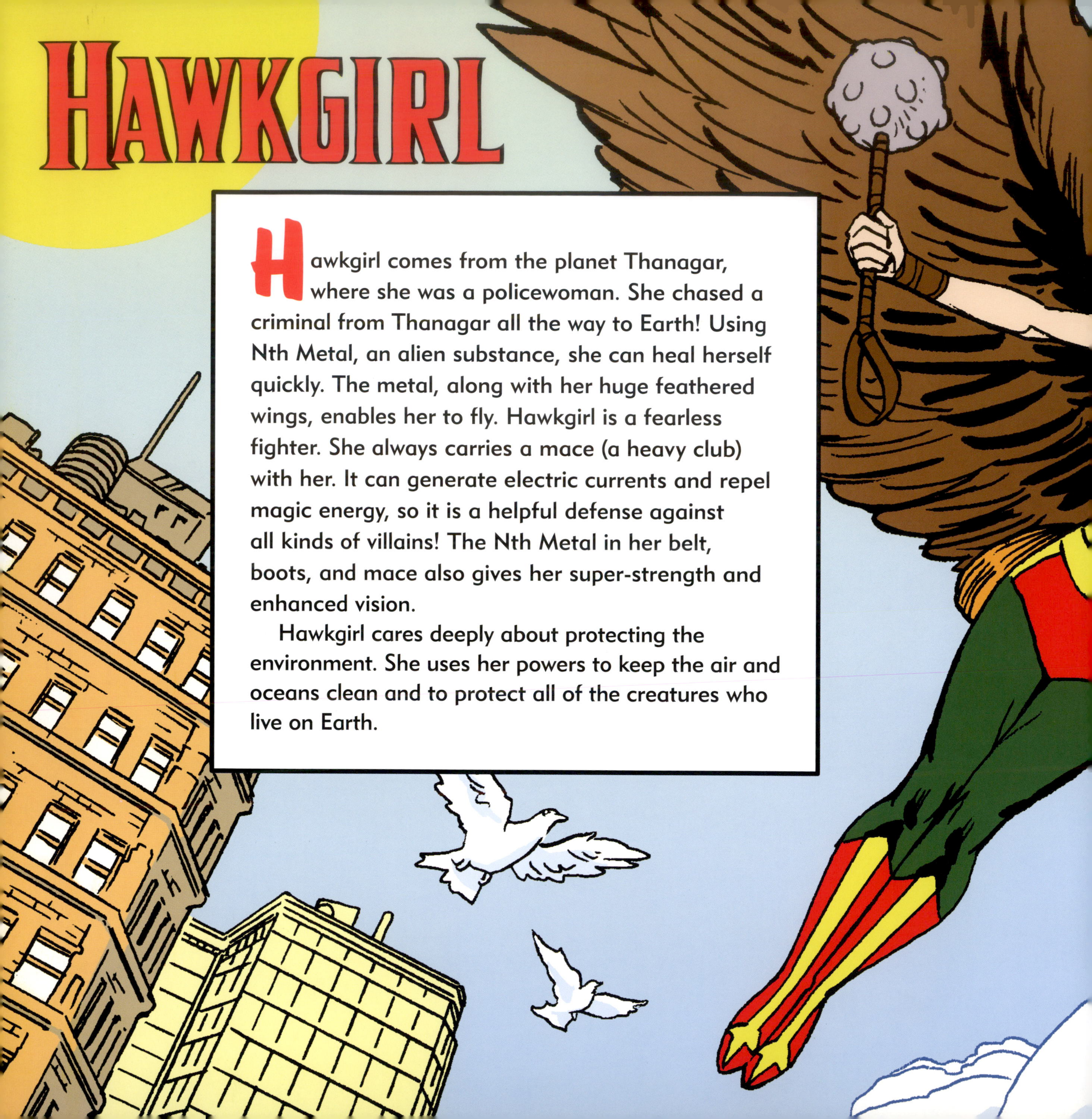

Hawkgirl comes from the planet Thanagar, where she was a policewoman. She chased a criminal from Thanagar all the way to Earth! Using Nth Metal, an alien substance, she can heal herself quickly. The metal, along with her huge feathered wings, enables her to fly. Hawkgirl is a fearless fighter. She always carries a mace (a heavy club) with her. It can generate electric currents and repel magic energy, so it is a helpful defense against all kinds of villains! The Nth Metal in her belt, boots, and mace also gives her super-strength and enhanced vision.

Hawkgirl cares deeply about protecting the environment. She uses her powers to keep the air and oceans clean and to protect all of the creatures who live on Earth.

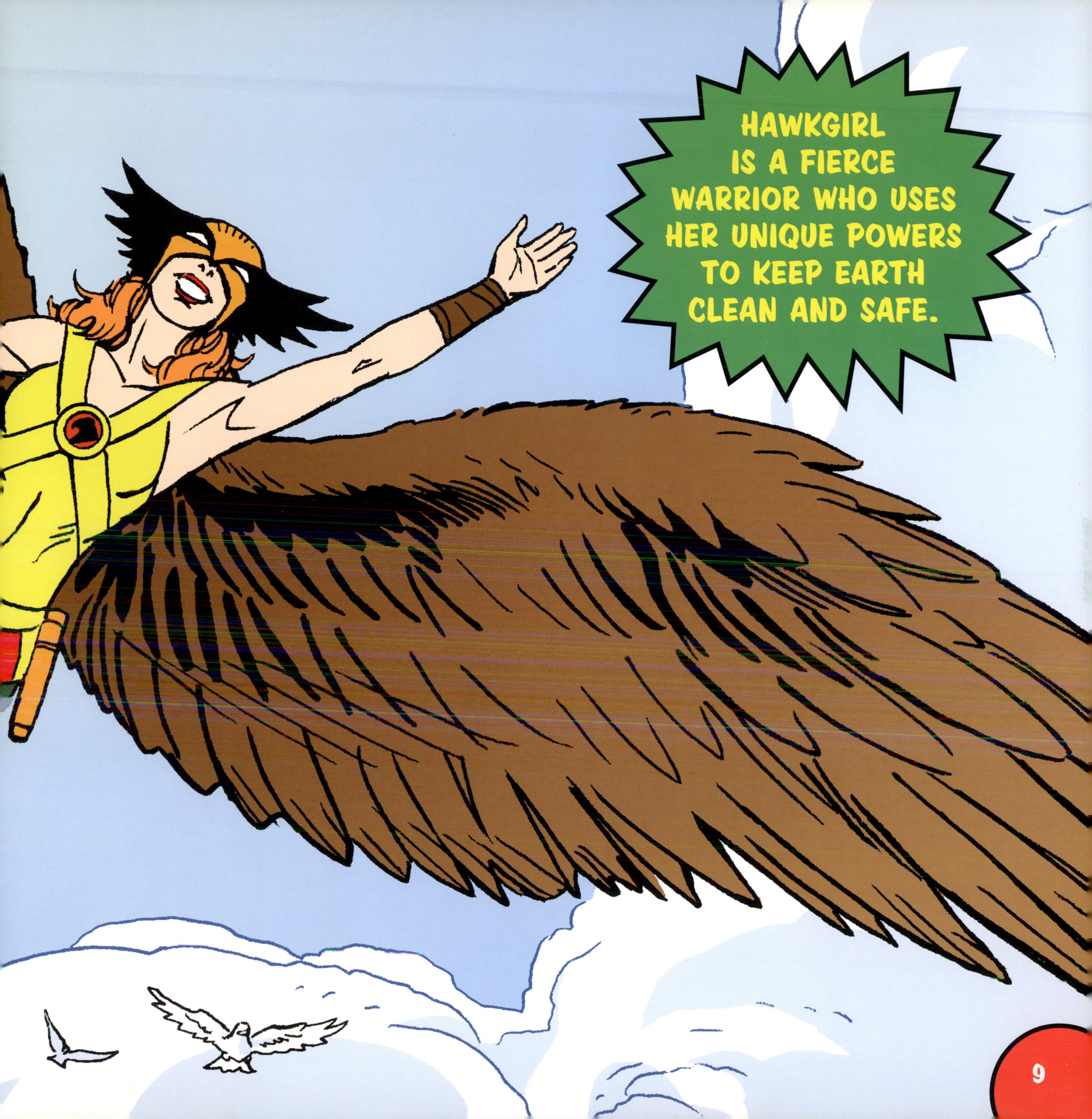
HAWKGIRL IS A FIERCE WARRIOR WHO USES HER UNIQUE POWERS TO KEEP EARTH CLEAN AND SAFE.

Bumblebee

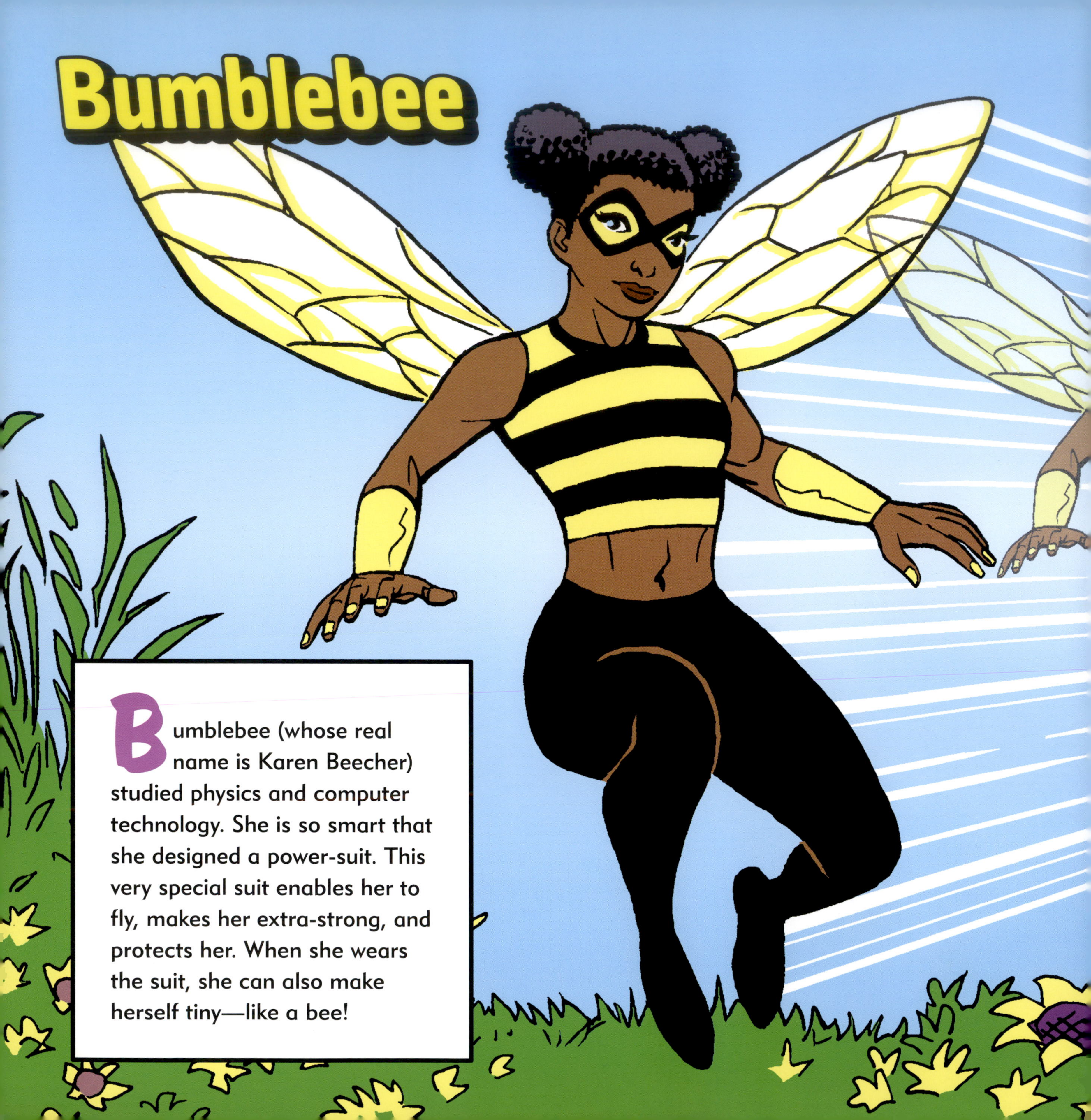

Bumblebee (whose real name is Karen Beecher) studied physics and computer technology. She is so smart that she designed a power-suit. This very special suit enables her to fly, makes her extra-strong, and protects her. When she wears the suit, she can also make herself tiny—like a bee!

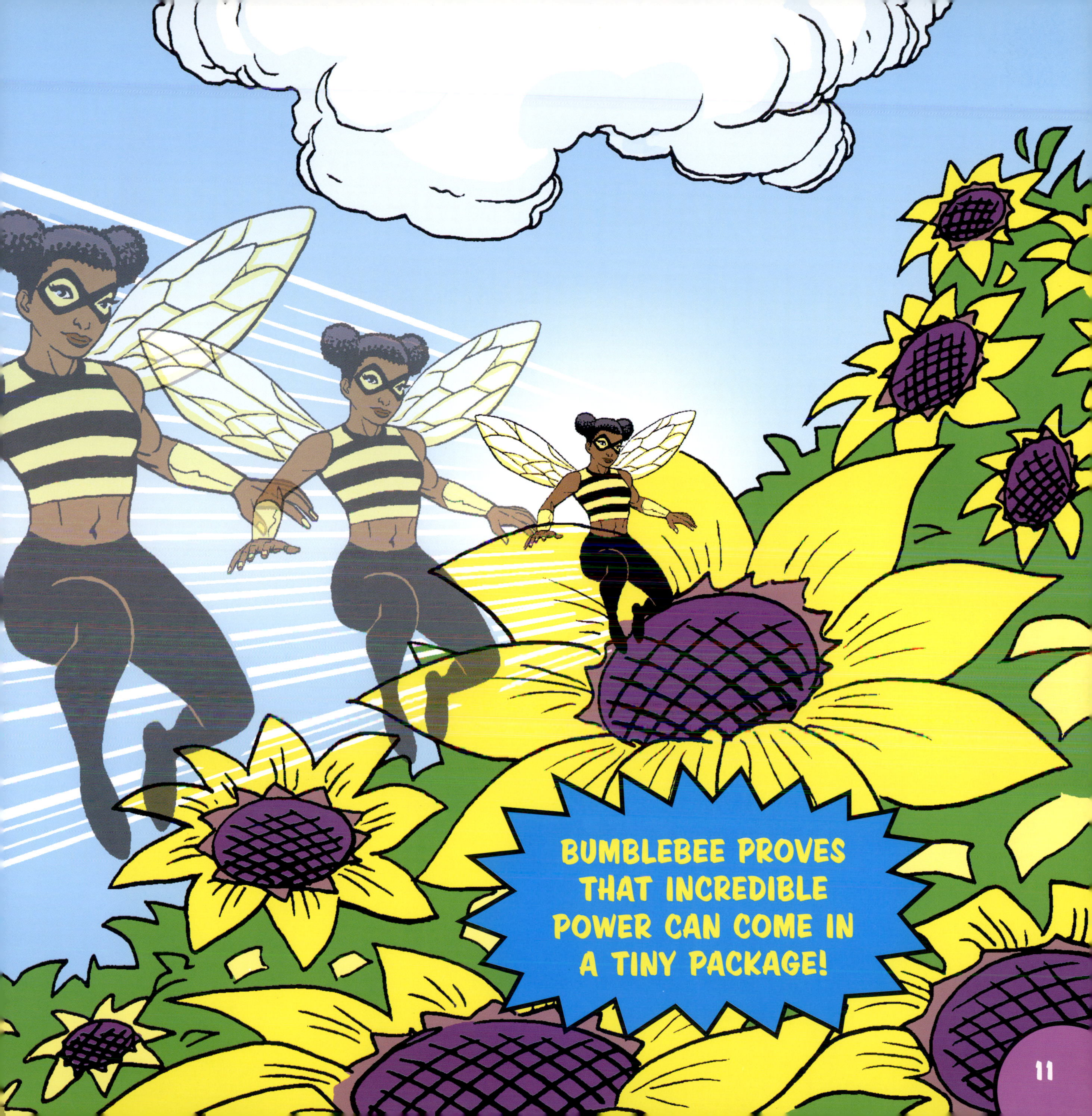
BUMBLEBEE PROVES
THAT INCREDIBLE
POWER CAN COME IN
A TINY PACKAGE!

CATWOMAN

Catwoman did not start out as a force for good.

At first, she was a thief! She was very sneaky and liked to steal. But then she started to feel bad about taking things that didn't belong to her. She decided to change her ways and start being helpful instead. She is a gifted athlete—a gymnast and acrobat who mastered karate and dragon-style kung fu!

Catwoman has a special relationship with cats. They seem to understand each other. Catwoman can calm and comfort scared or injured kitties.

Like a cat, Catwoman is speedy and agile. She can't fly like some of her friends, but she can jump from rooftop to rooftop. And she always lands on her feet.

Catwoman may not be a super hero, but she knows that it's important to help people (and kitties). She prowls the city at night, making sure her neighbors are safe.

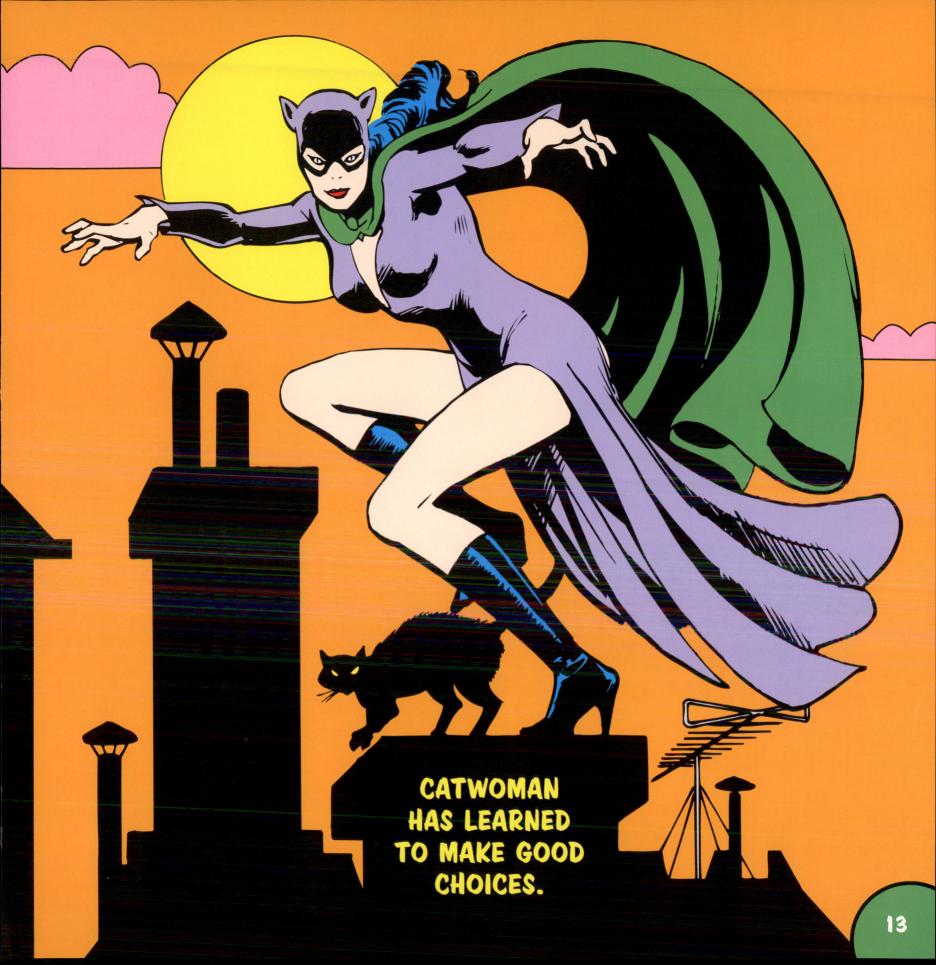

CATWOMAN
HAS LEARNED
TO MAKE GOOD
CHOICES.

13

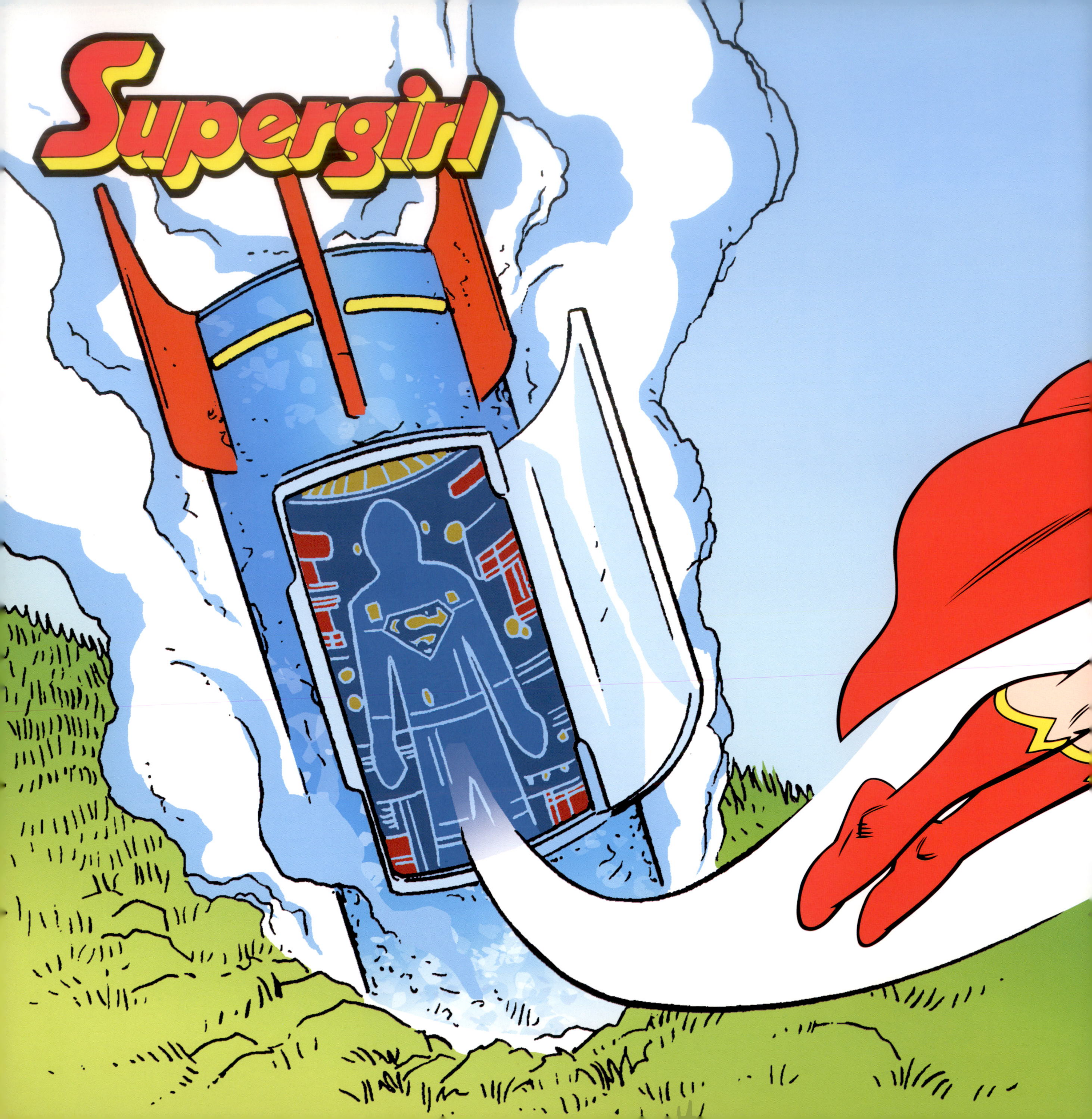
Supergirl

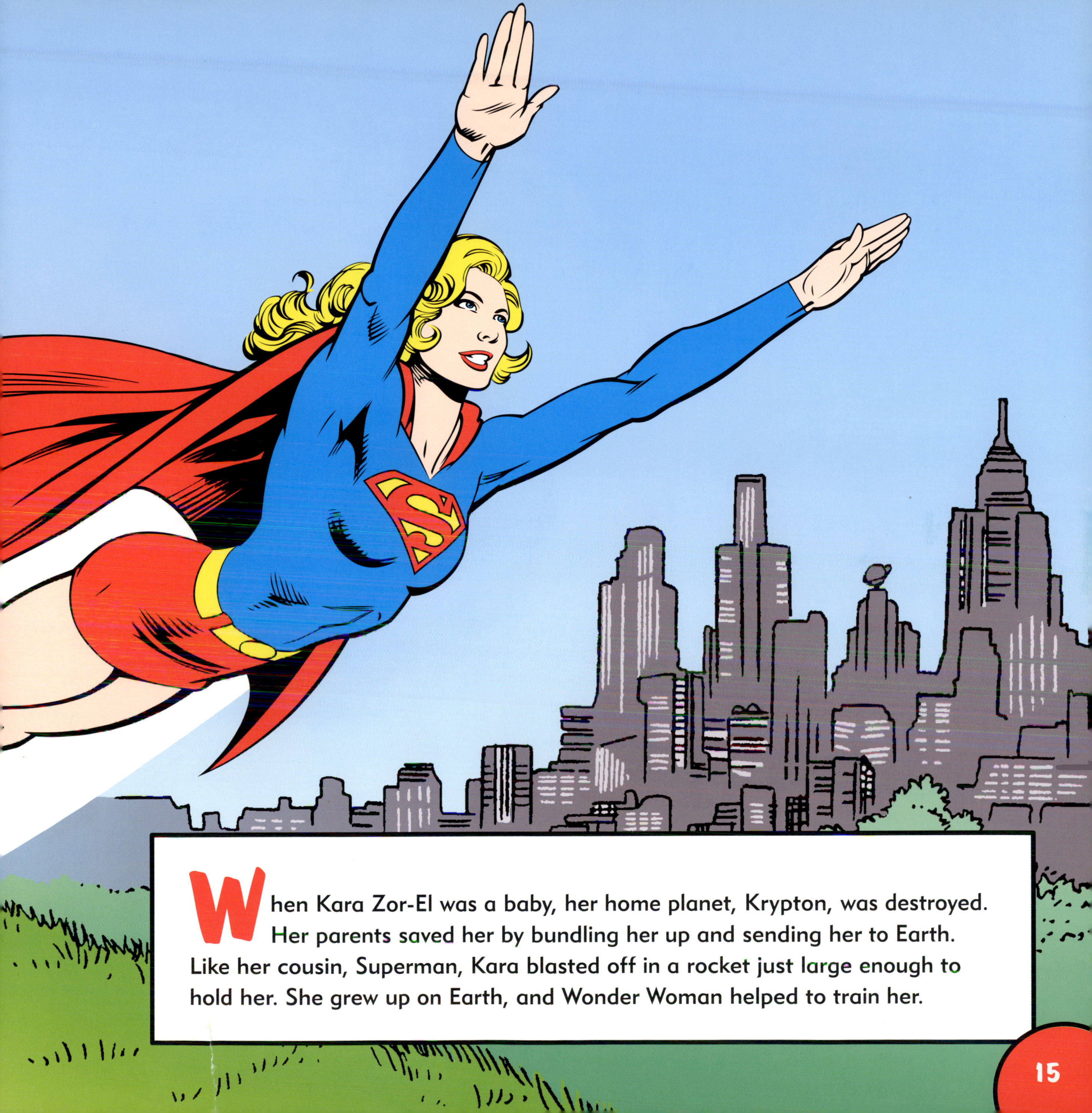

When Kara Zor-El was a baby, her home planet, Krypton, was destroyed. Her parents saved her by bundling her up and sending her to Earth. Like her cousin, Superman, Kara blasted off in a rocket just large enough to hold her. She grew up on Earth, and Wonder Woman helped to train her.

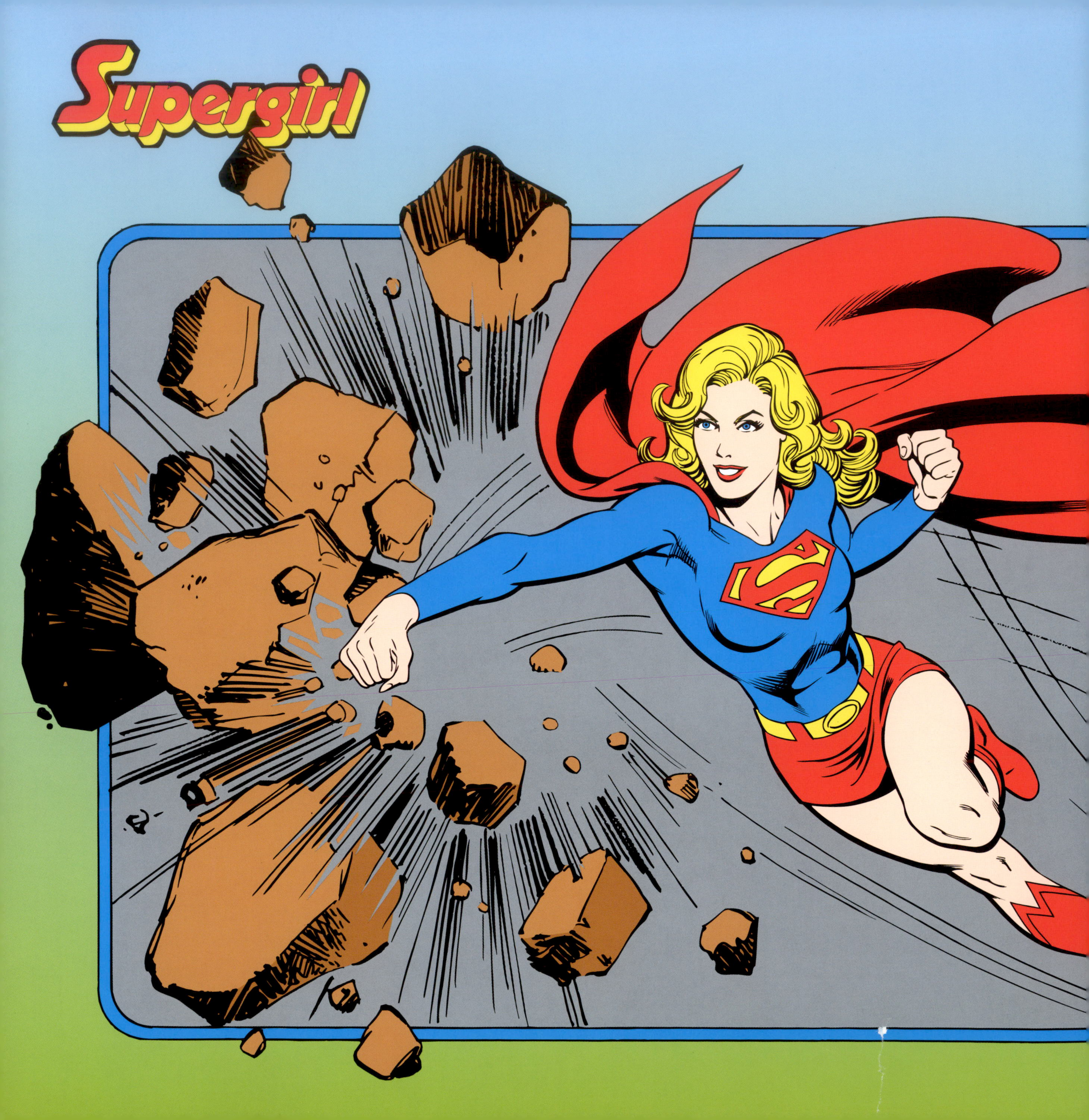
Supergirl

Like other Kryptonians, Supergirl is super-strong. She can shatter a solid wall with her fist or lift a whole stack of cars and throw them! Her X-ray vision lets her see through walls, and her heat vision can melt anything—even metal. She can also fly.

Supergirl uses her many special powers to protect people on Earth, her new home.

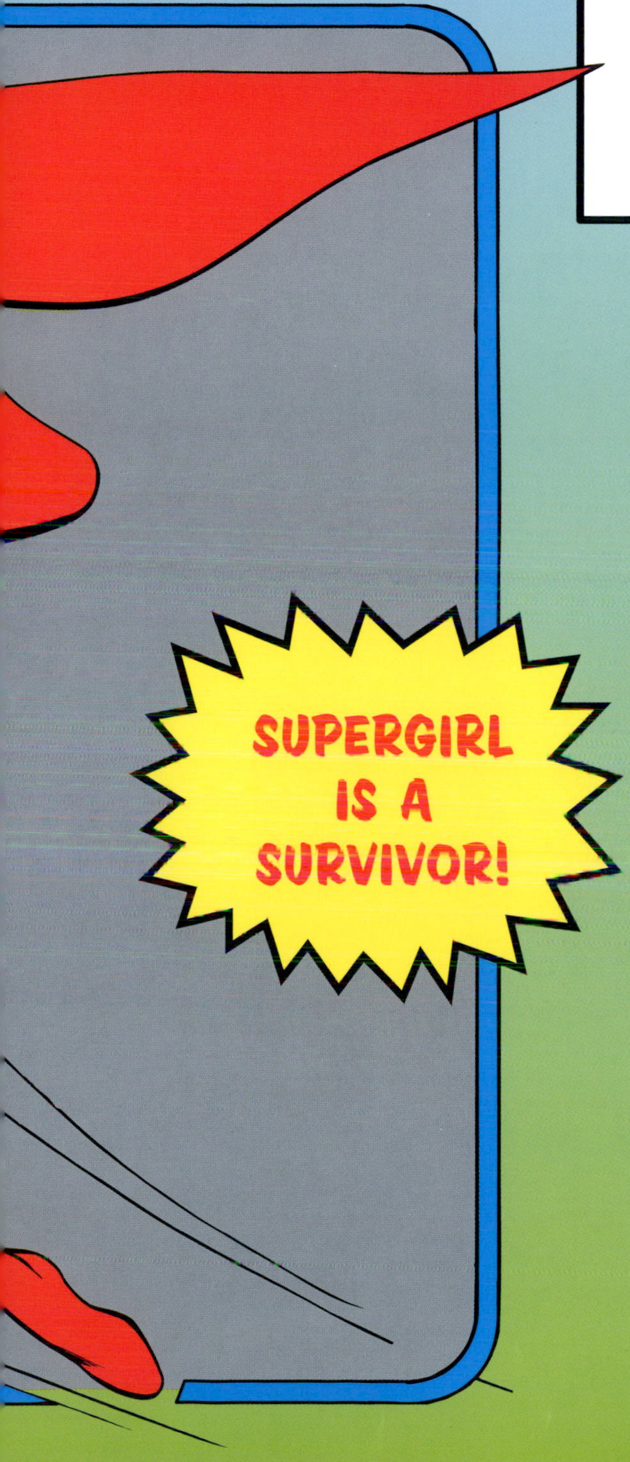
SUPERGIRL IS A SURVIVOR!

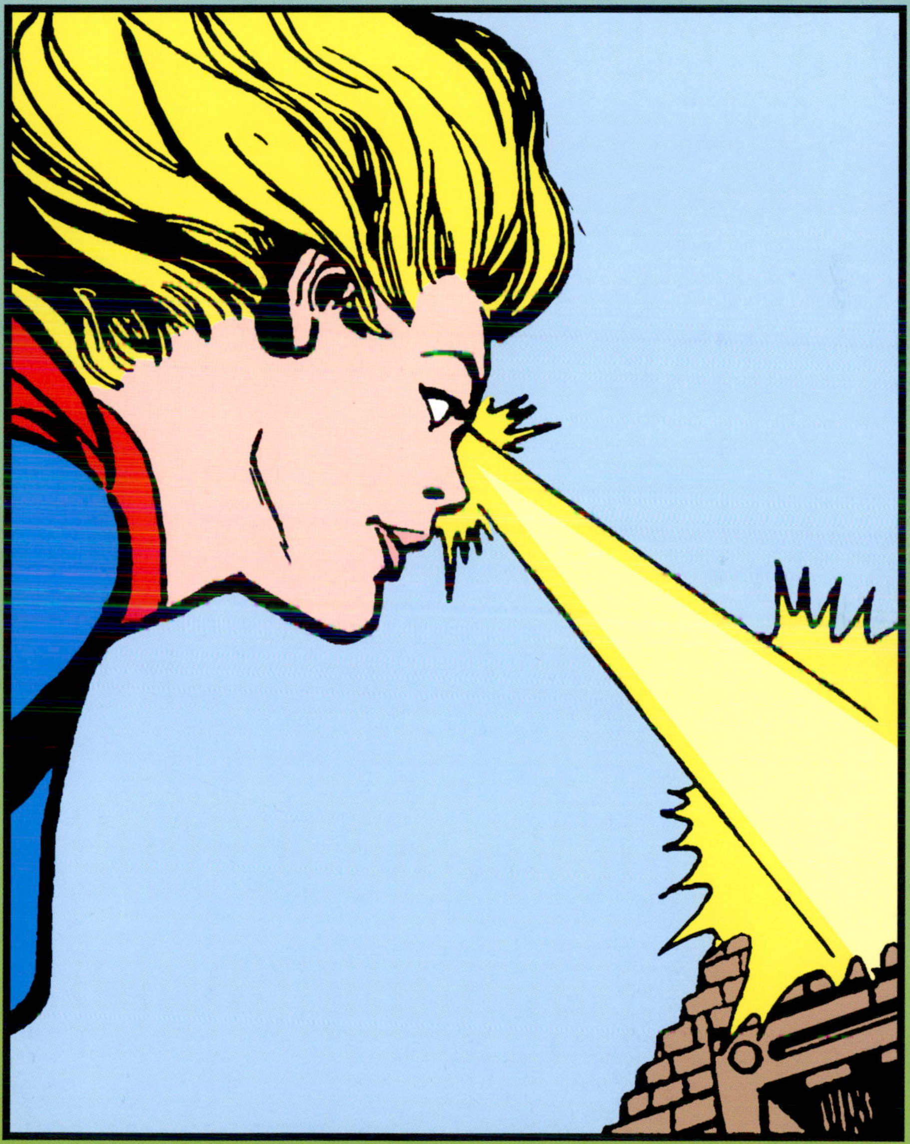

RAVEN

Raven grew up in a mystical place called Azarath. She has the power of empathy, which means that she can feel what other people are feeling—whether they are angry, joyful, or sad. She can also take away other people's pain.

Raven's power of telekinesis lets her move things with her mind. She could rescue a family from a fire by lifting them out of the flames with her mind powers!

Raven uses her magic powers to do good things.

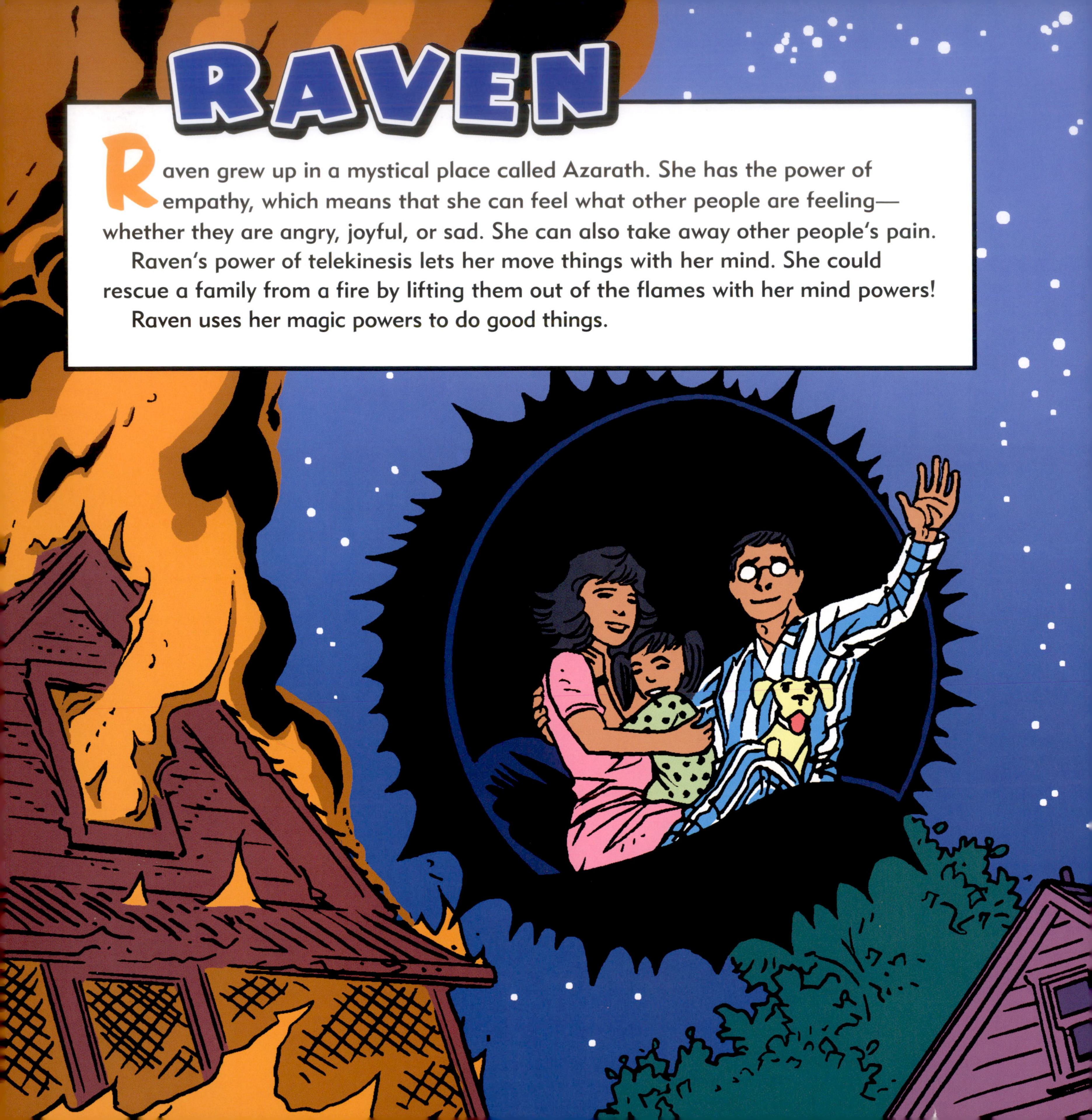

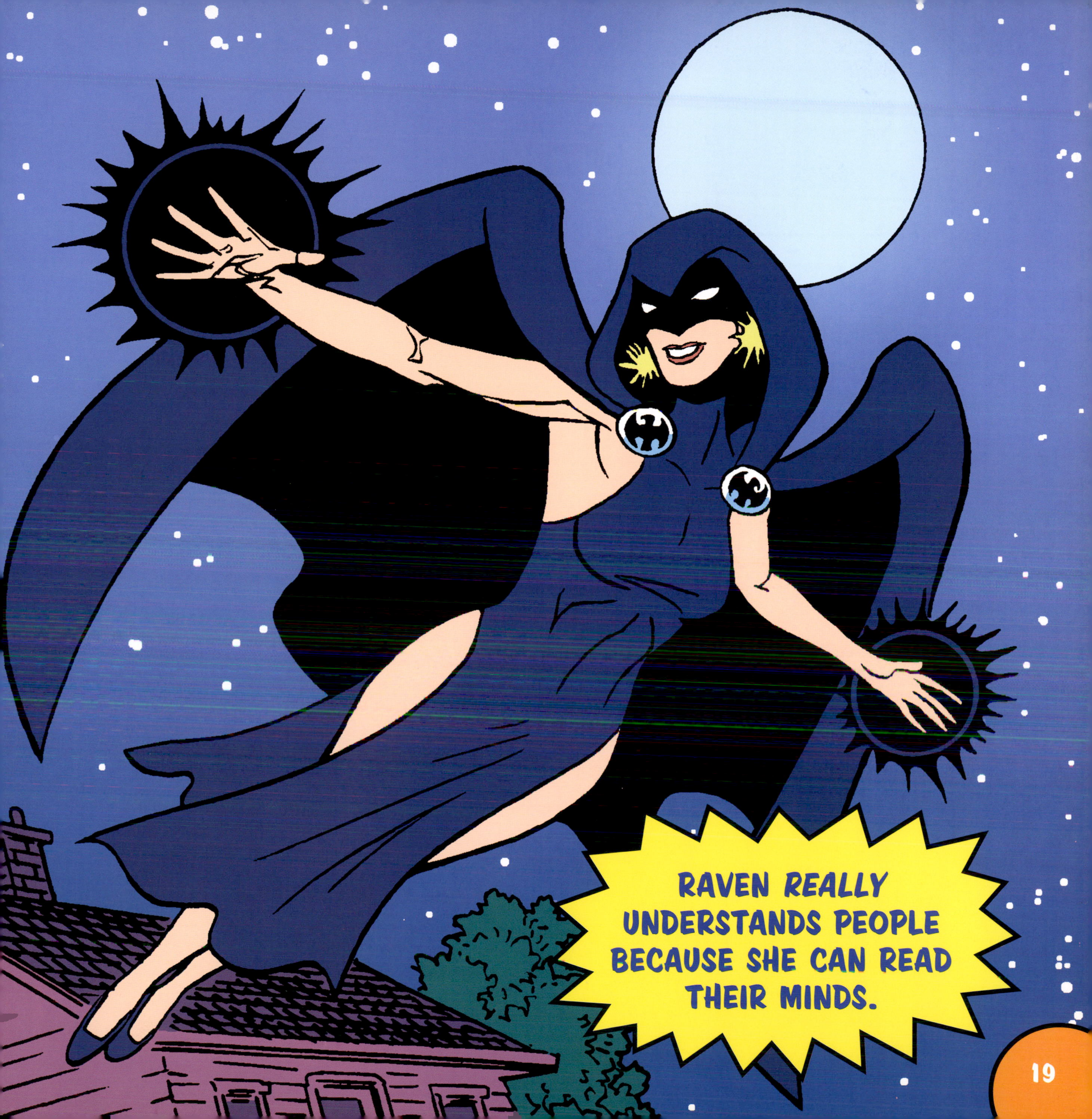
RAVEN *REALLY*
UNDERSTANDS PEOPLE
BECAUSE SHE CAN READ
THEIR MINDS.

Mera

Mera is the Queen of Atlantis, an undersea world. She can breathe both underwater and on land. She moves fearlessly between these worlds. Mera can swim much faster than any fish in the sea. And, on land, she can leap across huge distances—and even over buildings.

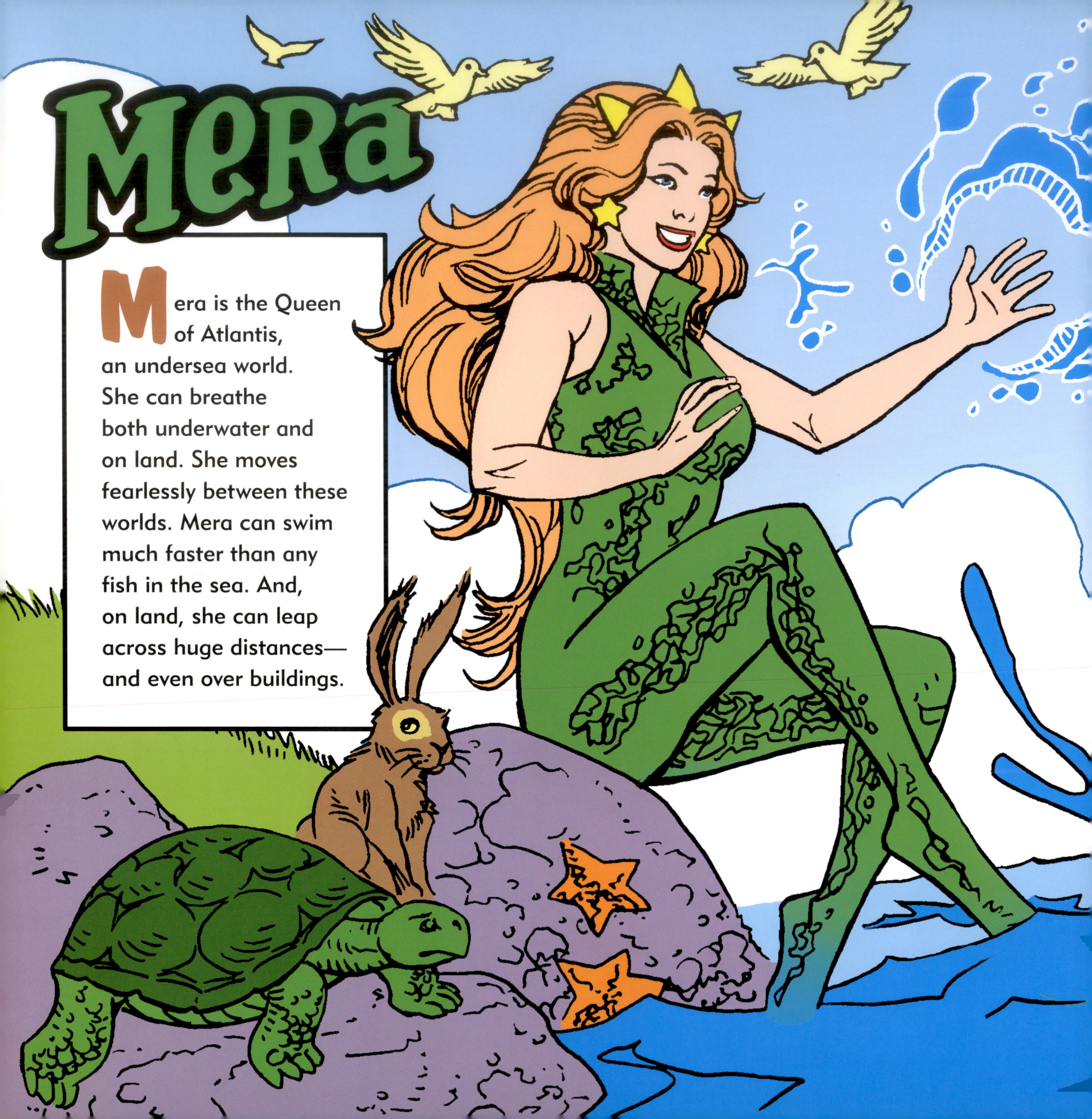

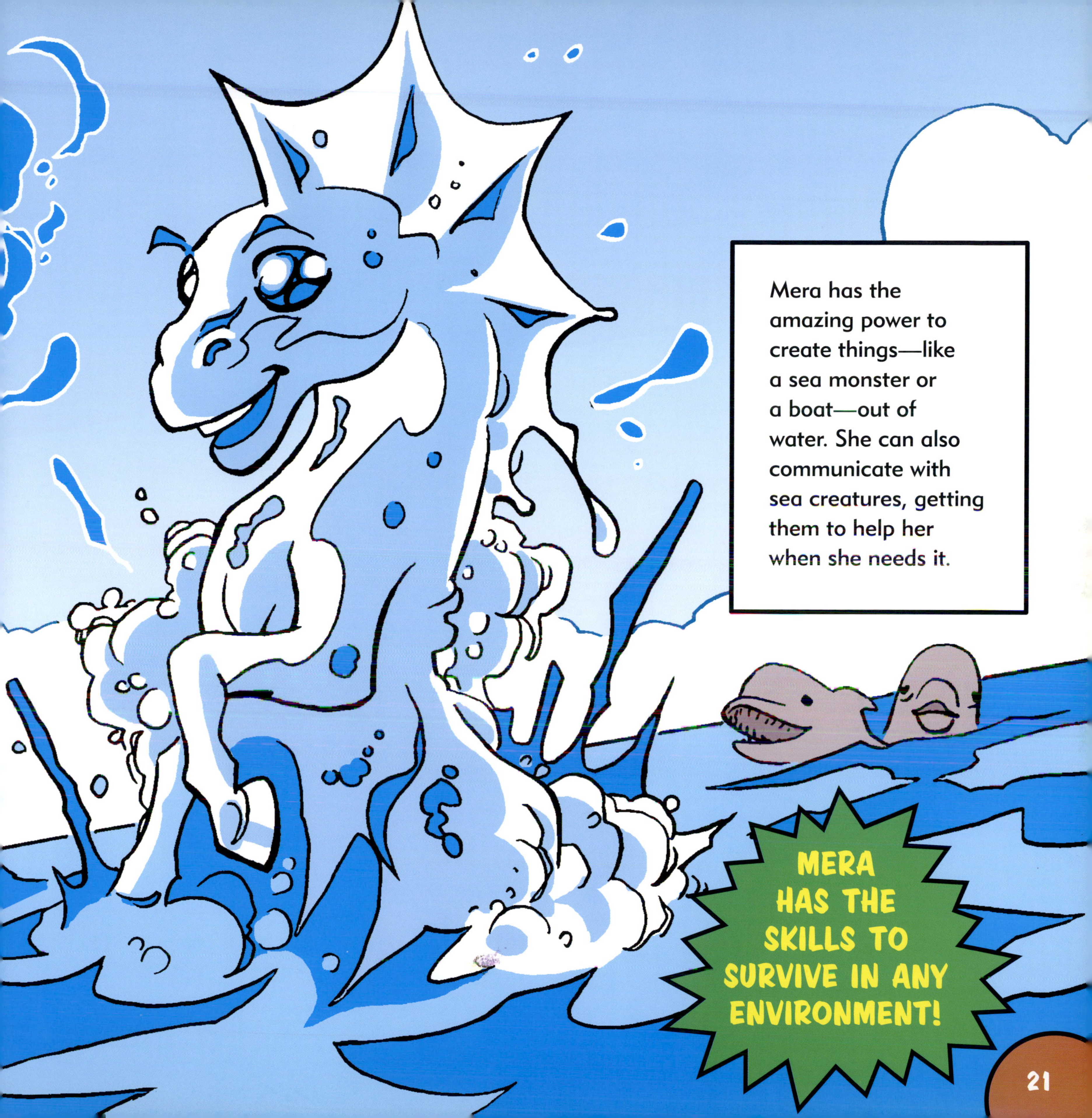
MERA HAS THE SKILLS TO SURVIVE IN ANY ENVIRONMENT!

Mera has the amazing power to create things—like a sea monster or a boat—out of water. She can also communicate with sea creatures, getting them to help her when she needs it.

STARFIRE

Starfire is not your average princess. She was born and raised on the planet Tamaran. When her planet was under attack, she made her way to Earth.

Like other Tamaraneans, she can convert light into power. When she uses this power to fly, she leaves a trail of light behind her.

Starfire also has the amazing ability to learn a new language just by touching someone who speaks that language. (She learned to speak English from Batman's sidekick, Robin!)

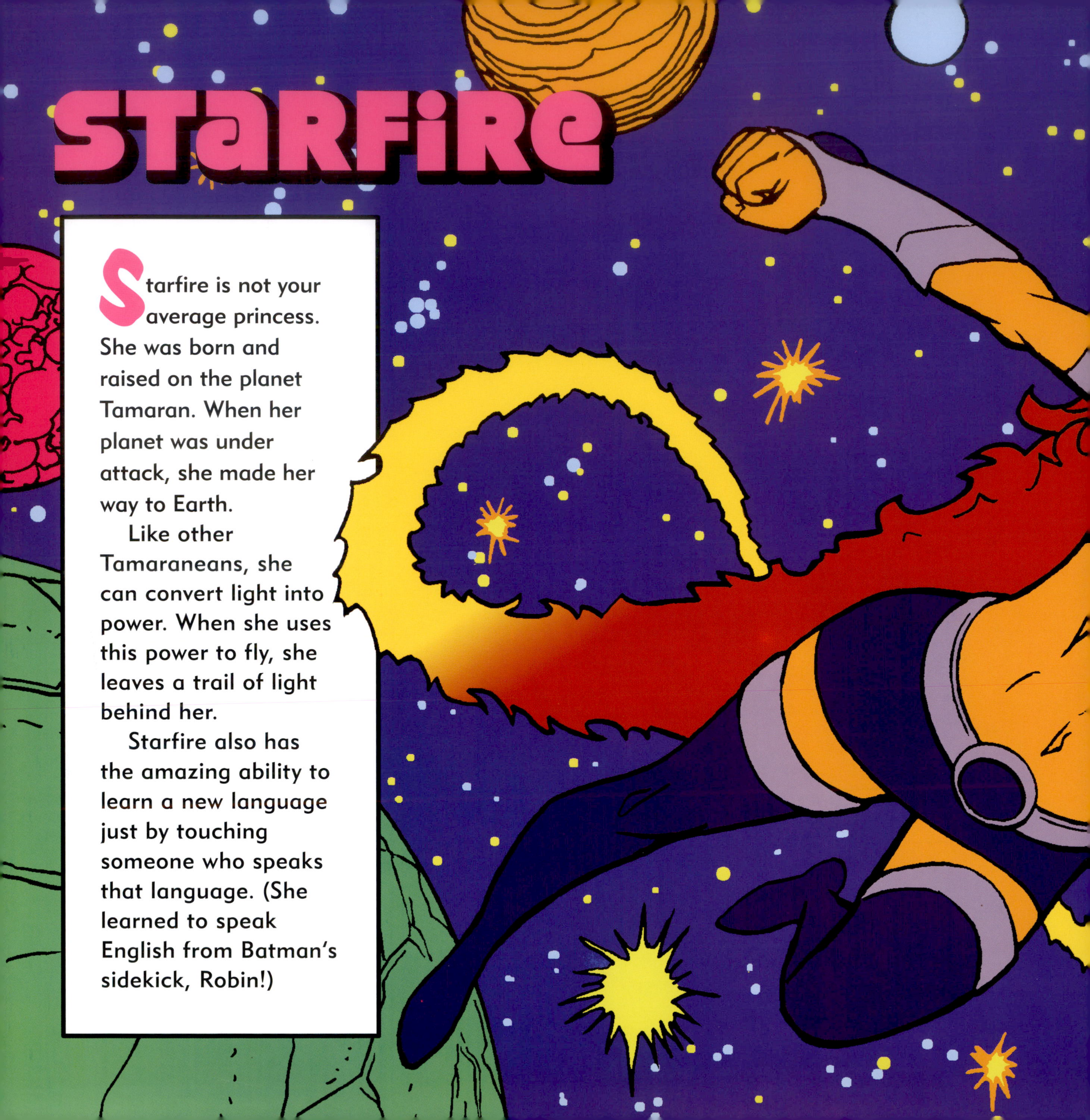

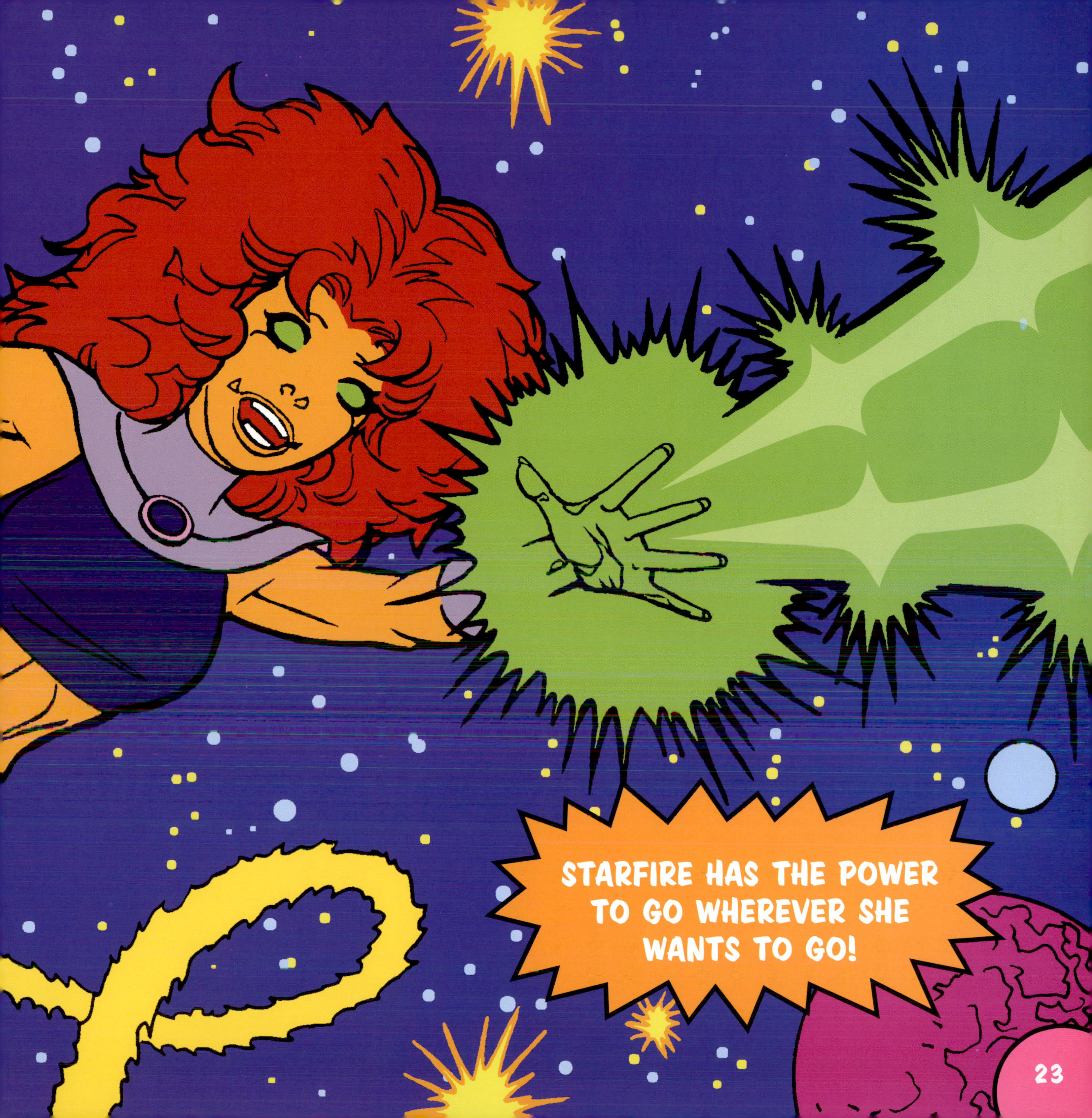
STARFIRE HAS THE POWER TO GO WHEREVER SHE WANTS TO GO!

Katana

Katana comes from Japan. When she was a young girl, she began to study martial arts. Martial arts are different types of self-defense—ways to protect yourself or even to fight others—using your body. Judo and karate are forms of martial arts.

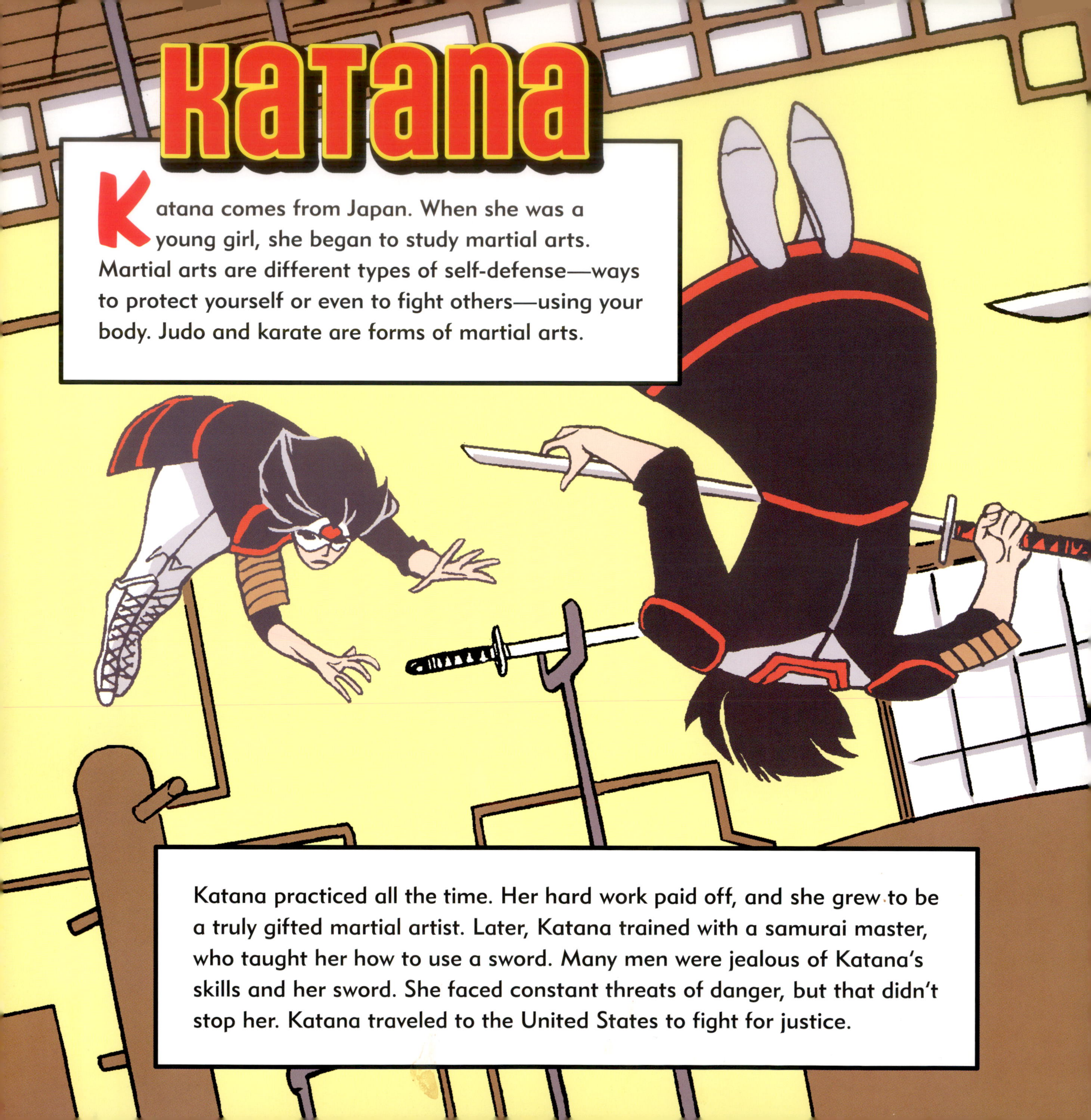

Katana practiced all the time. Her hard work paid off, and she grew to be a truly gifted martial artist. Later, Katana trained with a samurai master, who taught her how to use a sword. Many men were jealous of Katana's skills and her sword. She faced constant threats of danger, but that didn't stop her. Katana traveled to the United States to fight for justice.

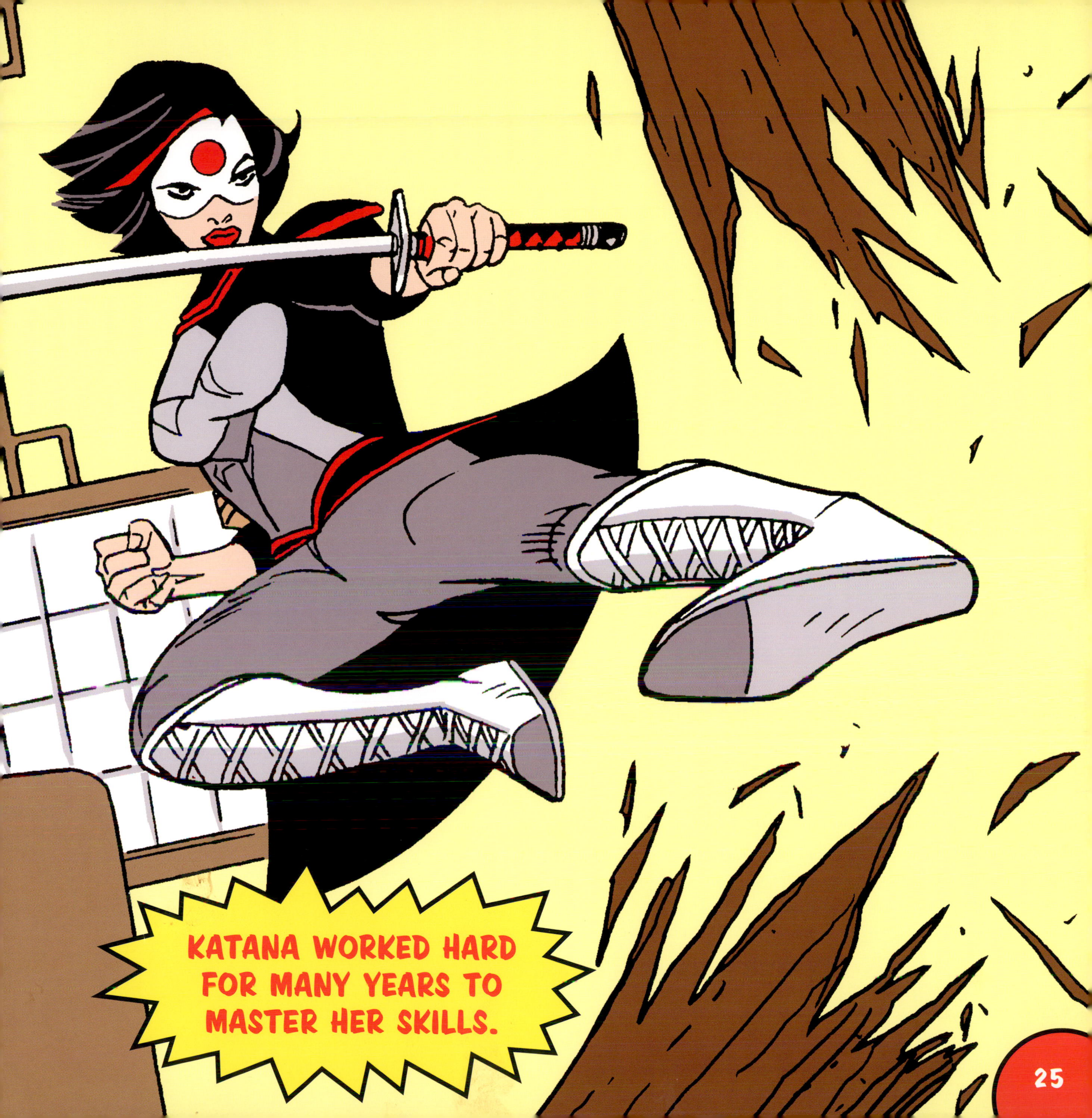
KATANA WORKED HARD FOR MANY YEARS TO MASTER HER SKILLS.

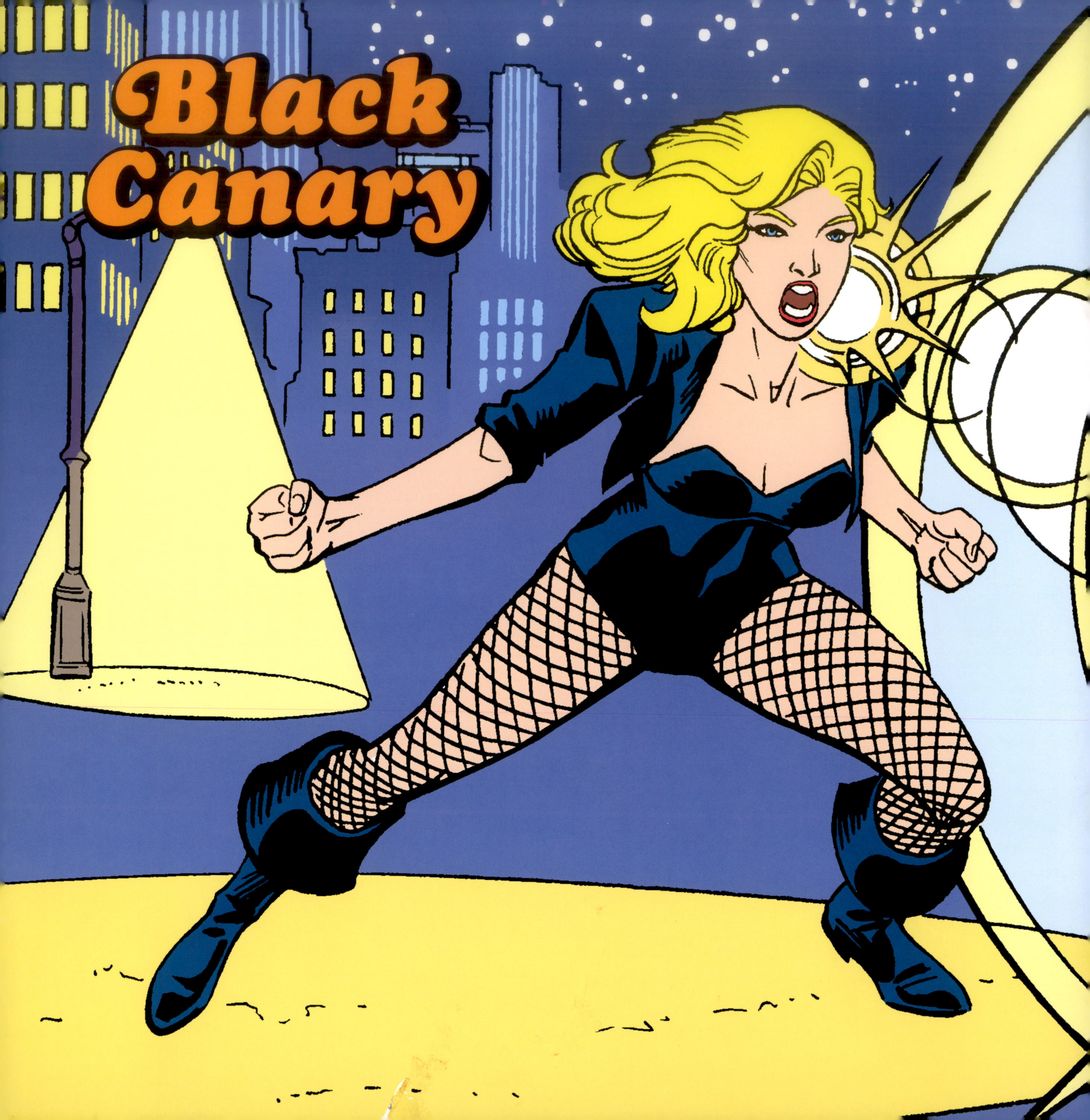
Black Canary

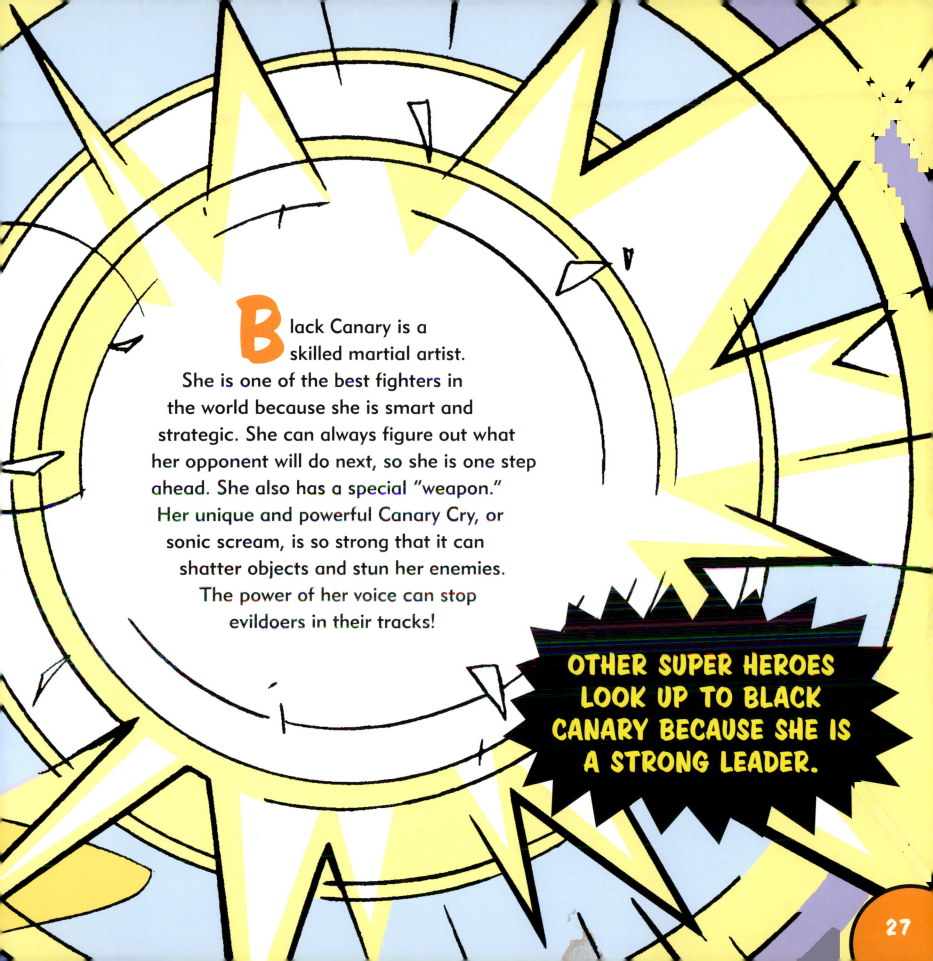

Black Canary is a skilled martial artist. She is one of the best fighters in the world because she is smart and strategic. She can always figure out what her opponent will do next, so she is one step ahead. She also has a special "weapon." Her unique and powerful Canary Cry, or sonic scream, is so strong that it can shatter objects and stun her enemies. The power of her voice can stop evildoers in their tracks!

OTHER SUPER HEROES LOOK UP TO BLACK CANARY BECAUSE SHE IS A STRONG LEADER.

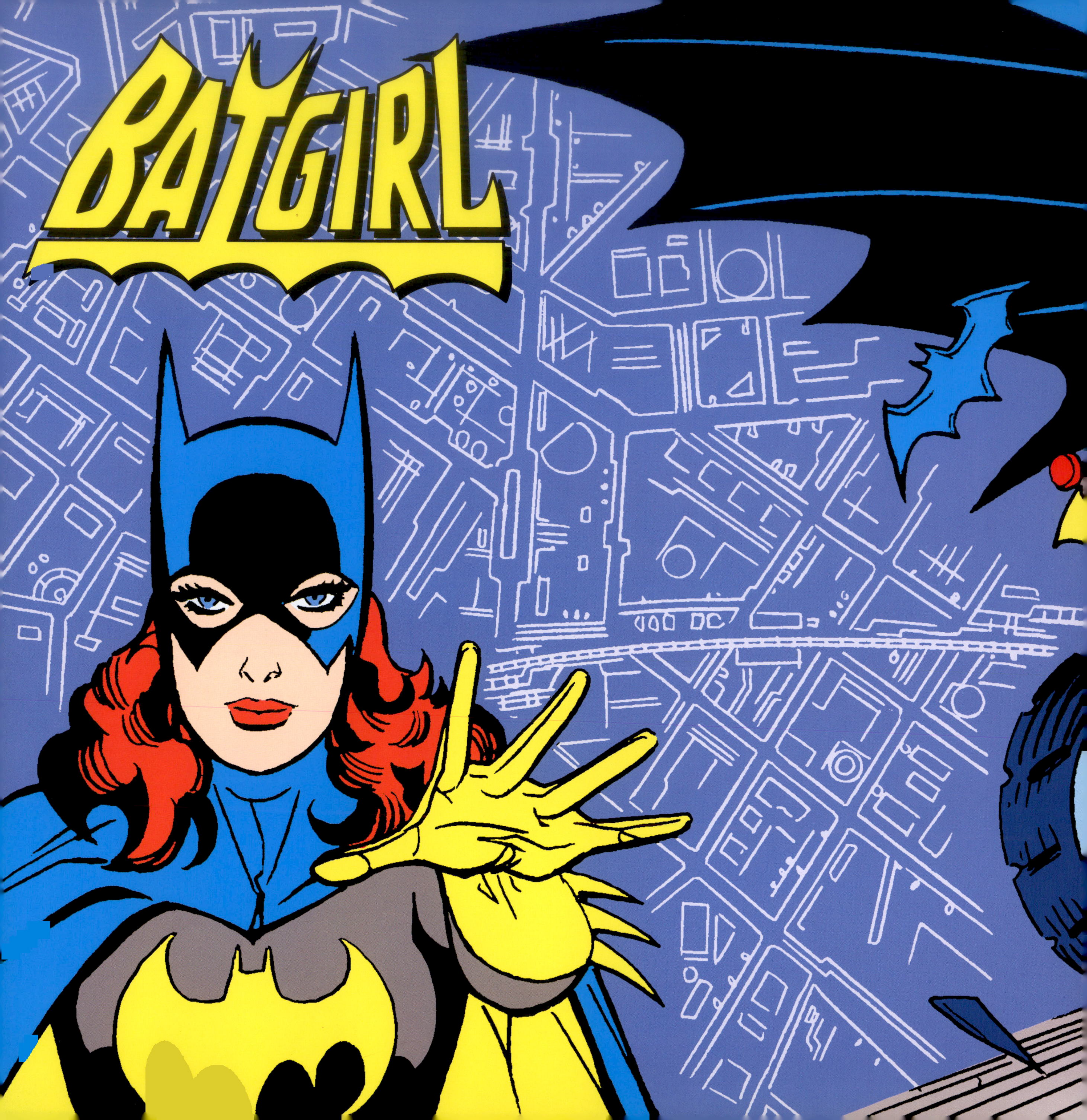
BATGIRL

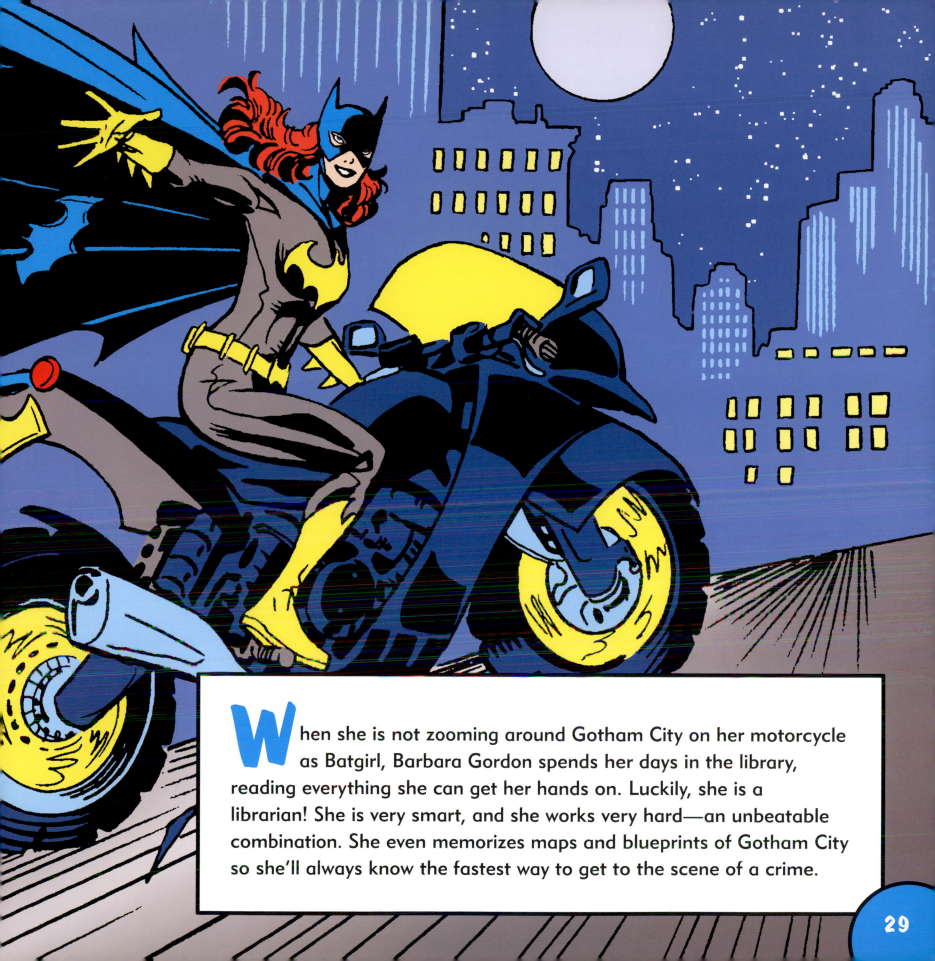

When she is not zooming around Gotham City on her motorcycle as Batgirl, Barbara Gordon spends her days in the library, reading everything she can get her hands on. Luckily, she is a librarian! She is very smart, and she works very hard—an unbeatable combination. She even memorizes maps and blueprints of Gotham City so she'll always know the fastest way to get to the scene of a crime.

As a young girl, Batgirl was a star athlete. Like her friend Katana, she studied martial arts. She became a technology whiz and can hack into computers if she needs to. Batgirl uses many gadgets, such as Batarangs and Batropes, to help her fight crime.

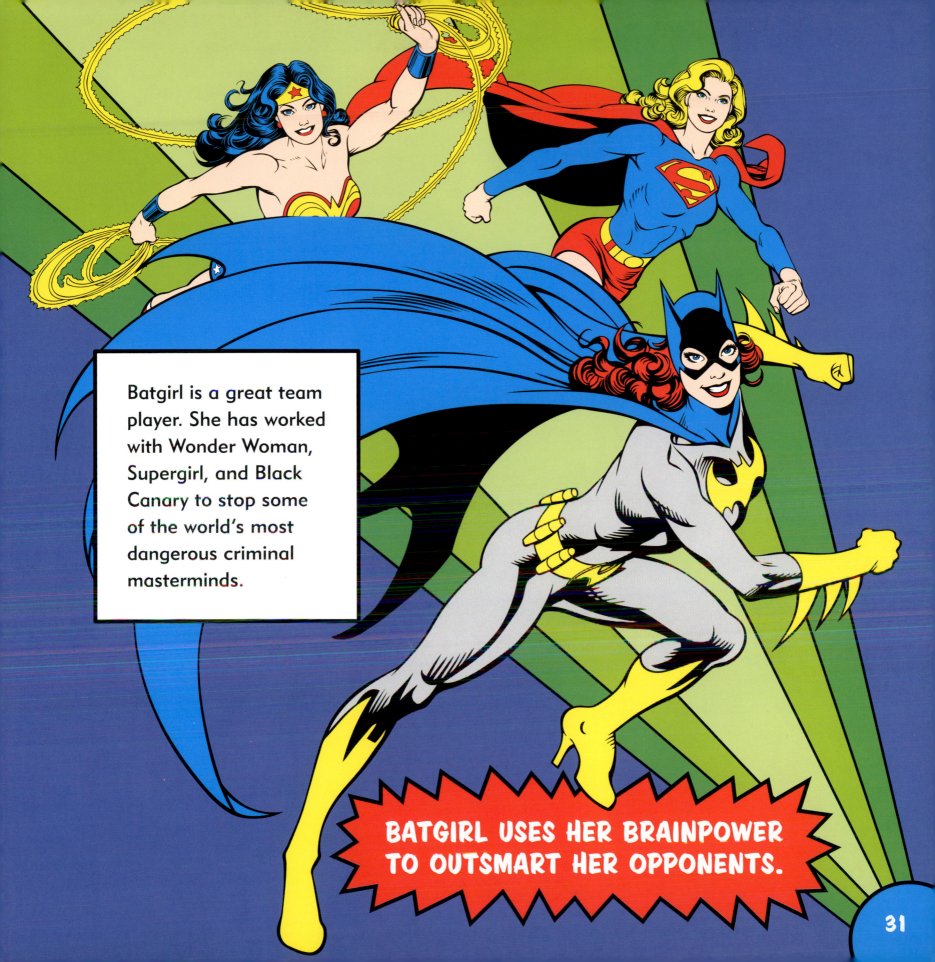

Batgirl is a great team player. She has worked with Wonder Woman, Supergirl, and Black Canary to stop some of the world's most dangerous criminal masterminds.

BATGIRL USES HER BRAINPOWER TO OUTSMART HER OPPONENTS.

When women get together to do good things, nothing and nobody can stop them!

What are your special powers? How will you use them to make the world a better place?

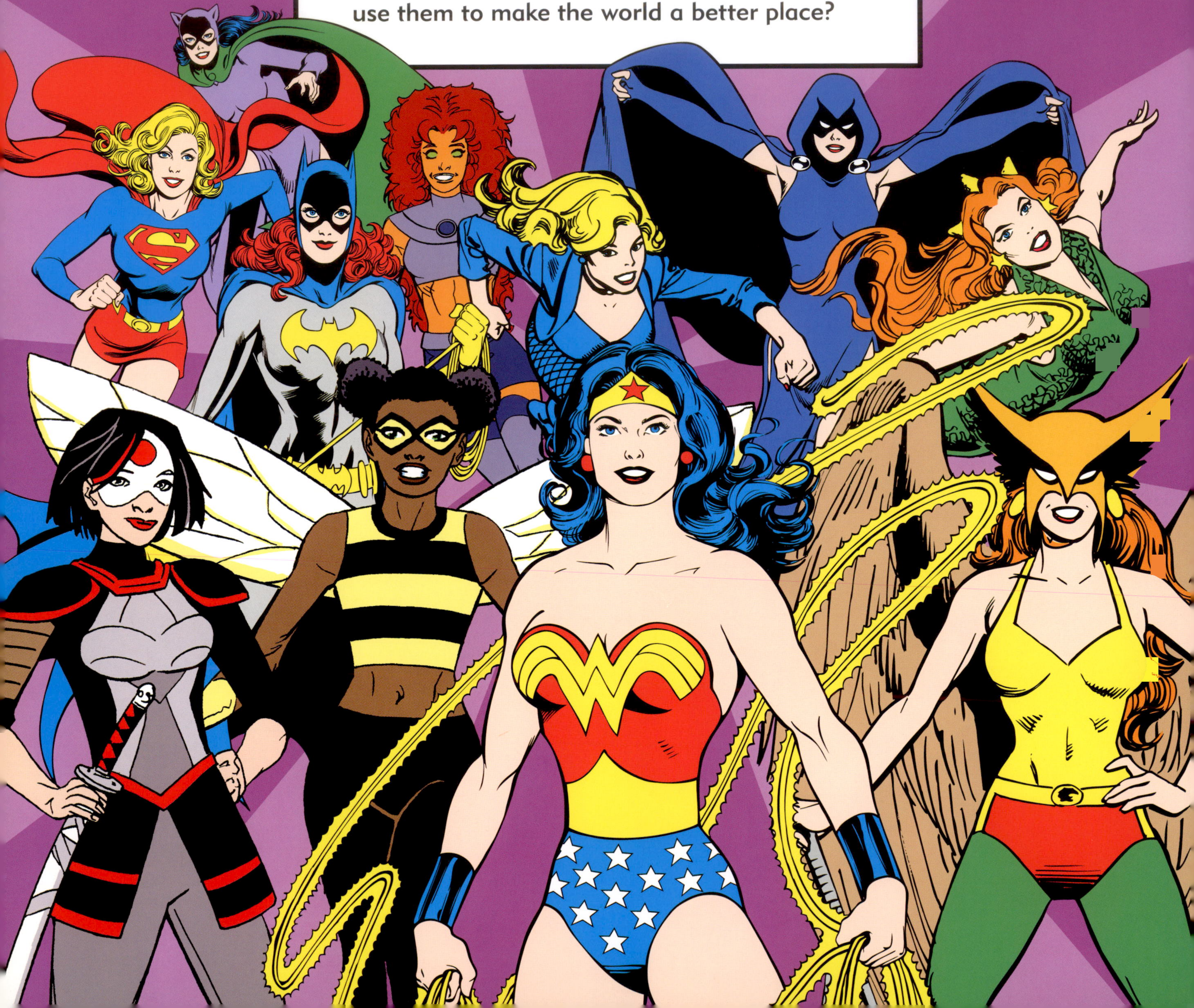

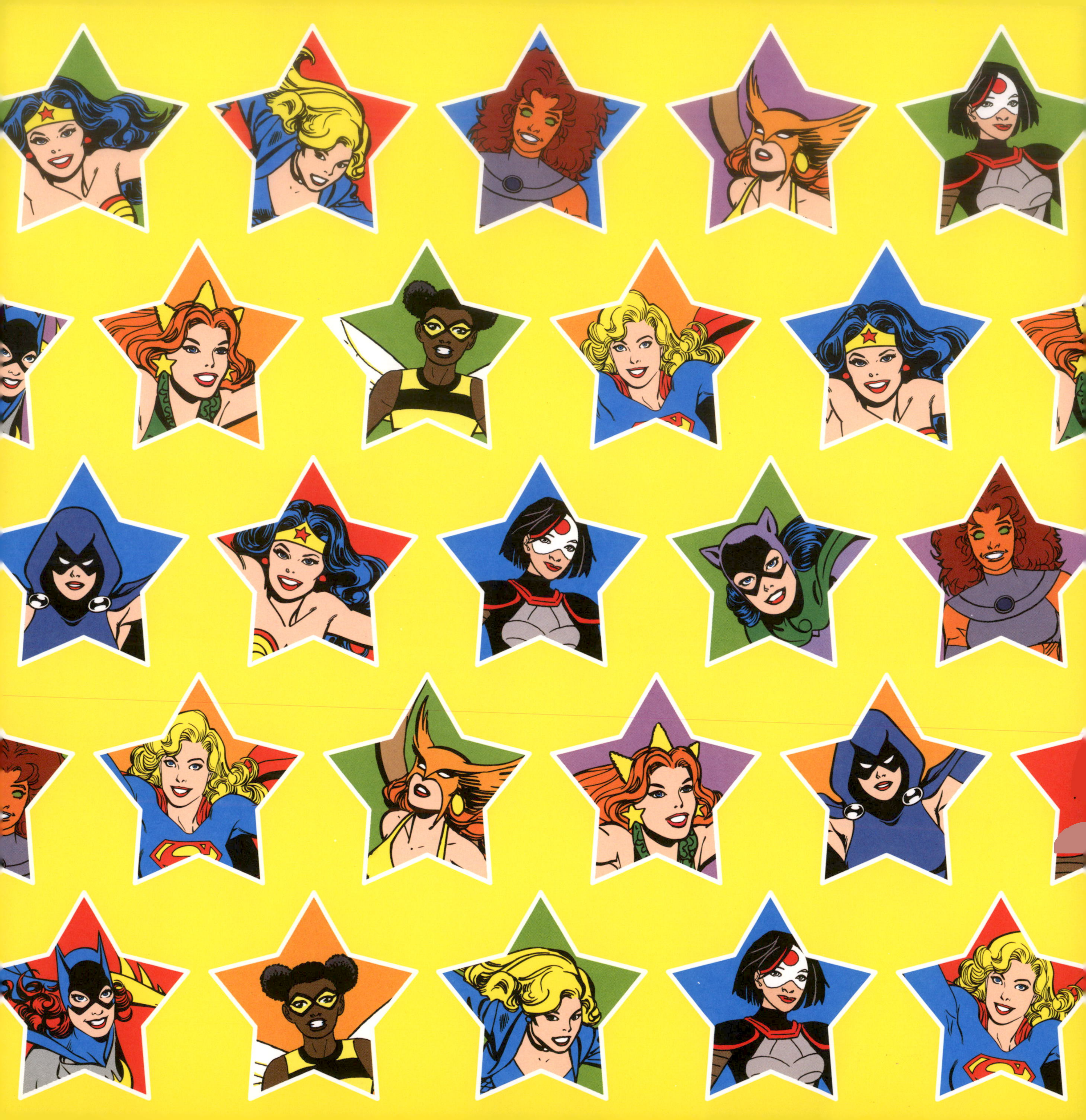